Perhaps if I wanted to be understood or to understand I would bamboozle myself into belief, but I am a reporter; God exists only for lead writers.

—*The Quiet American*, Graham Greene

A true war story is never moral. It does not instruct, nor encourage virtue, nor suggest models of proper human behavior, nor restrain men from doing the things men have always done. If a story seems moral, do not believe it.

—*The Things They Carried*, Tim O'Brien

A day with nice light, a cigarette, a war . . .

—*Comanche Territory*, Arturo Pérez-Reverte

To Gerda Taro, who spent one year at the Spanish front and who stayed on.

—*Death in the Making*, Robert Capa

SUSANA FORTES is a native of Spain. Her novels have been translated into almost twenty languages, and she is the winner of ~~literary awards, including the Premio Nuevos~~

Get **more** out of libraries

Please return or renew this item by the last date shown.
You can renew online at www.hants.gov.uk/library
Or by phoning 0300 555 1387

 Hampshire
County Council

SUSANA FORTES

Waiting for Robert Capa

Translation by Adriana V. López

Harper
Press

Harper*Press*
An imprint of HarperCollins*Publishers*
77–85 Fulham Palace Road
Hammersmith
London W6 8JB

This Harper*Press* edition published in 2012

Designed by Michael P. Correy

Printed and bound in Great Britain by
Clays Ltd, St Ives plc

MIX
Paper from
responsible sources
FSC
www.fsc.org   **FSC** C007454

Chapter One

It's always too late to turn back. Suddenly you wake up one day knowing that this will never end, that it will always be like this. Take the first train, make a quick decision. It's here or there. It's black or white. This one I can trust, this one I can't. Last night I dreamt I was in Leipzig at a gathering with Georg and everyone at the lake house, around a table covered in white linen, a vase of tulips, John Reed's book, and a pistol. I spent the whole night dreaming about that pistol and woke up with the taste of gunpowder in my throat."

The young woman closed the notebook on her lap and looked up at the scenery passing at a rapid speed outside her window; blue countryside between the Rhine and the Vosges mountains, villages with wooden houses, a rose bush, the ruins of a castle destroyed during one of the many medieval wars that devastated Alsace. This is how History enters us, she thought, not knowing that this very territory would soon return to being a battlefield. Battle tanks, medium-range Blenheim bombers, fighter biplanes, the German air force's Heinkel He 51s . . . The train passed in front of a cemetery and the other passengers in the compartment crossed themselves. It was difficult to fall asleep with all the wobbling. She kept hitting her temple against the window frame. She was tired. Closing her eyes, she could see her father bundled up in a thick cheviot coat, saying good-bye to her on the station platform at Leipzig. The muscles of his jawline shut tight, like a stevedore under a canopy of gray light. Grind teeth, clench fists inside pockets, and swear in a very low voice in Yiddish. That's what men who don't know how to cry do.

It's a question of character or principles. Emotions only worsen matters when the time comes to leave in a hurry. Her father always maintained a curious debate with tears. They were prohibited from crying as children. If the boys mixed themselves up in a fistfight, and lost in the scuffle, they could not return home to complain. A busted-up lip or a black eye was proof enough of their defeat. And crying was prohibited. The women didn't have to follow the same code of conduct, of course. But she loved her brothers and there was nothing in this world that would allow her to accept being treated differently. She was raised within those rules. So, there were no tears. Her father knew very well what he was saying.

He was old-fashioned, from Eastern Europe's Galicia, still using rubber-soled peasant shoes. As a child, she remembered his footprints alongside the farm's henhouse being as large as a buffalo's. His voice during the Sabbath ceremony in the synagogue was just as deep as his footprints in the garden. About two hundred pounds of depth.

Hebrew is an ancient language that contains the solitude of ruins within, like a voice from the hillside calling out to you, or the song of the siren heard on a distant ship. The music of the Psalms still moves her. She notices a cramp in her back when she hears it in dreams, like now, as the train travels to the other side of the border, a type of tickling sensation just below her side. Perhaps that's where the soul lives, she thought.

She never knew what the soul was. As a child, when they lived in Reutlingen, she believed that souls were the white diapers that her mother hung out to dry on the balcony. Oskar's soul. Karl's. Her own. But now she doesn't believe in those things. The God of Abraham and the twelve tribes of Israel would break her neck if they could. She did not owe them anything. She preferred English poetry a million times over. One poem by Eliot can free you from evil, she thought; God didn't even help me escape that Wächter-strasse prison.

It was true. She left by her own means, self-assured. Her captors must have thought that a blond girl, so young and so well-dressed, could not be a Communist. She thought it, too. Who would have known she would end up taking an interest in politics frequenting the tennis club in Waldau? A deep tan, white sweater, short pleated skirt . . . She liked the way exercise made her body feel, as well as dancing, wearing lipstick, donning a hat, using a cigarette holder, drinking champagne. Like Greta Garbo in *The Saga of Gosta Berling*.

Now the train had entered a tunnel, sounding a long whistle. It was completely dark. She breathed in a deep smell of railway emanating from the car.

She doesn't know exactly when everything started to twist itself. It happened without her realizing it. It was because of the damn cinders. One day the streets started smelling like a railroad station. It reeked of smoke, of leather. Well-polished high boots, saddlery, brown shirts, belt buckles, military trappings . . . One Tuesday, as she was leaving the movie theater with her friend Ruth, she saw a group of young men in the Weissenhof district singing the Nazi hymn. The boys were just pups. They did not pay it further mind.

Later, it was prohibited to buy anything in Jewish stores. She remembered her mother being thrown out of a gentile store, bending over to pick up her scarf that had fallen in the doorway as a result of the shopkeeper's push. That image was like a hematoma in her memory. A blue scarf speckled with snow. The burning of books and sheet music began around the same time. Afterward, the people began filling the arenas. Beautiful women, healthy men, honorable fathers with families. They weren't fanatics, but normal people, aspirin vendors, housewives, students, even disciples of Heidegger. They all listened closely to the speeches, they weren't being fooled. They knew what was happening. A choice had to be made and they chose. They chose it.

On March 18, at seven in the evening, she was detained by SA storm troopers at her parents' home. It rained. They came looking for Oskar and Karl, but since they did not find them, they took her instead.

Broken locks, open armoires, emptied-out drawers, papers everywhere . . . During the search they found the last letter Georg had sent from Italy. According to them, it spewed Bolshevik garbage. What did they expect from a Russian? Georg was never able to talk about love without resorting to the class struggle. At least he had been able to flee and was out of danger. She told them the truth, that she had met him at the university. He studied medicine in Leipzig. They were sort of boyfriend and girlfriend, but they gave each other their own space. He never accompanied her to parties her friends invited her to and she never asked about his gatherings until dawn. "I was never interested in politics," she told them. And she must have appeared convincing. One can suppose her attire helped. She wore the maroon skirt her aunt Terra had given her for graduation, high-heeled shoes, and a low-cut blouse, as if the SA had come to get her just as she was going out dancing. Her mother always said that dressing properly could save one's life. She was right. Nobody placed a hand on her.

As they drove through the corridors toward her cell, she heard the shouting coming from interrogations taking place in the west wing. When it was her turn, she played her part well. An innocent young woman, and frightened. In reality, she was. But not enough to stop her from thinking. Sometimes, staying alive solely depends on keeping your head in place and your senses alert. They threatened to keep her in prison until Karl and Oskar turned themselves in, but she was able to persuade them that she really couldn't supply them with any information. Choked voice, eyes wide-open, tender smile.

At night she stayed on her cot, silent, smoking, staring at the ceiling, her ego a bit bruised, wanting to end the whole charade once and for all. She thought about her brothers, praying that they'd been able to go underground, cross to Switzerland or Italy, like Georg. She also planned her escape for when she was able to get out of there. Germany was no longer her country. She wasn't thinking of a temporary escape, but of starting a new life. All the languages she learned would have to come of some use. She had to find a way out. She'd do it. That she was sure of. This is why she had a star. The train came back out into the light again as the wagon clattered through the mountains. They had entered another landscape. A river, a farm surrounded by apple trees, hamlets with chimneys blowing smoke. Children playing on top of an embankment lifted their arms toward the edge of dusk, moving their hands from left to right as the train abandoned the last curve.

The first shooting star she saw was in Reutlingen, when she was five years old. They were walking back from their neighbor Jakob's bakery with a poppy-seed cake and condensed milk for dinner. Karl was ahead, kicking rocks; she and Oskar always lagged behind, and so Karl, with his big-brother finger, pointed to the sky.

"Look, Little Trout." He always called her that. "Make a wish." Up there darkness was the color of prunes. Three little children, interlinking arms over shoulders, looking up at the sky, while they fell, two by two, three by three, like a handful of salt, those stars. Even now, when she remembers it, she can smell the wool from the sweater sleeves on her shoulders.

"Comets are a gift of good luck," said Oskar.

"Like a birthday present?" she asked.

"Better. Because it's forever."

There are things that siblings just know, the kinds of details spies use to confirm identities. Memories that slither beneath the tall grass of childhood.

Karl was always the smartest of the three. He taught her how to behave if she were ever arrested and to use the secret codes of communication that the Young Communists used, like pounding out the letters to the alphabet through the walls. This, at least, helped earn her the respect of her fellow prisoners. In order to survive in prison, one must reinforce the mechanisms of mutual aid as much as possible. The more you know, the more you are worth. Oskar, on the other hand, explained to her how to build one's inner strength for resistance. How to hide weakness, act with the utmost assurance, self-confidence. So that your emotions don't betray you. One can smell fear, he'd tell her. You have to see it coming.

She looked around with suspicion. There was a passenger in her compartment, smoking cigarette after cigarette. He was dressed in black. In order to let some air into the compartment, he opened the window and propped his arms up on the pane. A very light rain spritzed her hair and refreshed her skin. I can smell him, she thought. He's here, at my side. You have to think faster than they do, evaporate into the air, disappear, slip out, disappear however you can, become someone else, he told her. That's how she learned how to create characters, just like she did when she was an adolescent playing with her friend Ruth in the attic, imitating silent-film actresses, posing provocatively, holding imaginary long-stemmed cigarettes between her fingers. Asta Nielsen and Greta Garbo. Surviving is escaping toward what's next.

After two weeks, they let her go. April 4. There was a red dahlia and an open book on the windowsill. Her family's efforts by way of the Polish consul proved effective. But she always believed that if she was let out of there, it was because of her star.

It is not a metaphor to feel the constellations' influence on the world, and neither is questioning a mineral's incredible precision for always pointing toward the magnetic pole. The stars have guided cartographers and sailors for millennia, sending messages for millions of light-years. If sound waves travel through the ether, then somewhere in the galaxy there must also be the Psalms, litanies, and prayers of men floating within the stars.

Yahweh, Elohim, Siod, Brausen, whoever you are, lord of the plagues and of the oceans, ruler of chaos and of annihilated masses, master of chance and destruction, save me. Entering beneath the iron arc of the Gare de l'Est station, the train made its way to the platform. On the other side of the window, a world of passengers on their daily commute. The young woman opened her notebook and began writing.

"When you don't have a world to go home to, one has to trust their luck. Sangfroid and a capacity to improvise. These are my weapons. I've been using them since I was a little girl. That's why I'm still alive. My name is Gerta Pohorylle. I was born in Stuttgart, but I'm a Jewish citizen with a Polish passport. I've just arrived to Paris, I'm twenty-four years old, and I'm alive."

Chapter Two

The doorbell rang and she stood frozen before the kitchen oven, holding her breath, with the teapot still in hand. She wasn't expecting anyone. In the dormer window, a gray cloud squashed the rooftops along the Rue Lobineau. The glass was broken and a strip of adhesive tape, which Ruth had carefully placed, still lay over it. They had shared that apartment since she first arrived in Paris.

Gerta bit her lip until it bled a little. She thought the fear had passed, but no. That was one thing she learned. That fear, the real kind, once it has installed itself into the body, never goes away. It remains there, crouched in the form of apprehension, though there is no longer any motive, and one finds themselves safe in a city of rooftops with dormers, free of jail cells where someone can be beaten to death. It was as if there was always a step missing on the staircase. I know this sensation, she said to herself, the rhythm of her breathing returning to normal, as if the adrenaline rush had tempered her will. The fear was now splattered across the tiles of their kitchen floor where she'd spilled her tea. She recognized it in the way you recognize an old traveling companion. Always knowing their whereabouts. You there. Me here. Each in their own place. Maybe it should be like this, she thought. When the loud ring of the doorbell sounded a second time, she placed the teapot on the table in slow motion, and prepared herself to open the door.

A thin young man with a hint of fuzz over his lip tilted toward her in a kind of bow before handing her a letter. It was in a long envelope, without any official postmarks but the Refugee Help Center's blue-and-red stamp. Her name and address were written in all caps. As she opened the flap, she noticed the blood in her temples pulsing, slowly, like the accused must feel awaiting the verdict. Guilty. Innocent. She couldn't quite understand what the letter said. And had to read it several times until the rigidness in her muscles subsided and the expression on her face began to change like the sun when it appears from behind a cloud. It wasn't that she smiled, but that she was now smiling on the inside. It took over all the factions of her face, not only her lips but her eyes as well: her way of looking up at the ceiling as if the wings of an angel were fluttering above. There are things that only siblings know how to say. And once they say them, the entire universe shifts, everything is put back into its place. The passage of an adventure novel read out loud by children on porch steps before dinner can contain a secret code whose meaning no one else can interpret. That's why when Gerta read, "Beneath his eyes, bathed in moonlight, lay a fortified enclosure, from which rose two cathedrals, three palaces, and an arsenal," she could feel the heat from the oil lamp's flame heading up the sleeves of her blouse. It illuminated the cover illustration of a man with his hands tied, walking behind a black horse being ridden by a Tartar over snow-covered lands. That's when she knew with all certainty that the river was the Moscow River, the walled territory was the Kremlin, and that the city was Moscow. Just as it was described in the first chapter of *Michael Strogoff.* And she was at ease, because she understood that Oskar and Karl were safe.

The news filled her insides with energy, a kind of vital exhilaration that she needed to express immediately. She wanted to tell Ruth, Willi, and everyone else. She looked at herself in the moon that covered the door of the wardrobe. Hands deep in pockets, hair blond and short around the face, arched eyebrows. She was studying herself in a thoughtful and careful manner, as if she had just come face-to-face with a stranger. A woman barely five feet tall, with a tiny and muscular body similar to a jockey's. Not overly pretty, not overly smart, just another of the 25,000 refugees that arrived in Paris that year. The cuffs of her rolled-up shirtsleeves over her arms, the gray pants, bony chin. She moved closer to the mirror and saw something in her eyes, a kind of involuntary obstinacy that she didn't know how to interpret, nor did she want to. She limited herself to taking out a lipstick from the nightstand drawer, opening her mouth, and quickly outlining her smile in a fiery red bordering on shameless.

Sometimes you can find yourself hundreds of miles from home, in an attic in the Latin Quarter, with water stains on the ceiling and pipes that sound like the foghorn of a ship, not knowing what will become of your life. Without residency papers, and with little money except for when your friends in Stuttgart can find a way of shipping some over to you. You discover the oldest reasons for uprooting, feel the same desolation in your soul as all those who have been obliged to travel the longest thousand miles of their lives and look at themselves afterward in the mirror and discover that, despite it all, a desire to be happy is written on their faces. An enthusiastic resolution, irreducible, void of cracks. Perhaps, she thought, this smile will be my only safe-conduct. In those days, the reddest lips in all of Paris.

In a hurry, she grabbed her trench coat from the coat rack and went out into the morning of the streets.

For months now, the city of the Seine was a hotbed of thoughts and opinions, a place conducive to the bravest and brightest ideas. Montparnasse cafés, open at all hours, became the center of the world for the newly arrived. Addresses were exchanged, job opportunities sought, the latest news from Germany discussed, and every now and again one could get hold of a Berlin newspaper to read. In order to get a summary of the day's news, it was customary to go from table to table along all the stops on the route. Gerta and Ruth would often make a date to meet at Le Dôme Café's outside patio, and it was precisely where Gerta was headed. Walking in her peculiar way, hands in the pockets of her trench coat, shoulders hunched from the cold chill as she crossed the Seine. She enjoyed that ashen light, the generous schedules, the lead gutters on the roofs, the open windows, and the world's ideas.

But Paris was not only that. Many considered the flood of refugees a burden. "The Parisians will embrace you and then leave you shivering in the street," Ruth liked to say, and she was right. As it was done before in Berlin, Budapest, and Vienna, the fate of European Jews was now being written on the city's walls. While passing in front of the Austerlitz station, where she was supposed to pick up a package, Gerta saw a group of young men from the Croix-de-Feu putting up anti-Semitic posters in the station, and before she knew it, night had fallen. Again, a bitter smell of gunpowder rose to her throat. It was unexpected and different from the fear that she had experienced at home when the doorbell rang. It was more like an uncontrollable eruption. A reckless sensation that caused her to scream, coarse and loud, with a voice that did not resemble her own in the least.

"Fascistes! Fils de pute!"

The rebuke was heard loud and clear, in perfect French. That's exactly what she said. There were five of them. All were wearing leather jackets and high boots, like cocks with their spurs. *But where the hell was her self-assurance and sang froid?* She had her regrets when it was already too late. An older man exiting the door from the post office looked her up and down with disapproval. The French, always so restrained.

The tallest one of the group became defiant and began walking toward her, taking big strides. She could have found safe haven in a store, café, or in the very post office, but she didn't. It did not occur to her. She simply changed direction, cutting the corner onto a narrow street with balconies looming above. She walked, trying not to accelerate the pace, instinctively protecting herself by holding her handbag tightly over her abdomen. Aware of the footsteps behind her. Cautious. Without turning around to look. When she had barely made it around the entire block, she was able to perfectly hear, word for word, what the individual on her trail had directed at her. A voice as cutting as a handsaw. And that's when she started running. As fast as she could. Without caring about where she was going, as if her running had nothing to do with the threat she'd just heard but with another reason. Something inside, blocking her, as if she were being held captive in a labyrinth. And she was. Her mouth was dry, and she felt a pang of shame and humiliation heading up her esophagus, like the time when she was a child at school and her classmates poked fun at her customs. She went back to being that little girl in a white blouse and plaid skirt, forbidden to touch coins during the Sabbath. Someone who, deep down in her soul and with all her might, hated being Jewish, because it made her vulnerable. Being Jewish was a blue scarf speckled with snow in a doorway of a spice shop, her mother crouched over and keeping her head low. Now she was dodging the passersby she was brusquely meeting head-on, making them do a double-take: a young woman in such a rush could only be trying to escape herself. She took a quick left onto a passageway with gray mansard roofs and a smell of cauliflower soup that turned her stomach. And there she had no choice but to stop. At a corner, she grabbed onto a lead gutter and vomited all the tea from breakfast.

It was after twelve when she finally arrived at Le Dôme Café. Her skin moist with sweat, her hair wet and pushed back.

"What on earth happened to you?" asked Ruth.

With shoulders hunched, Gerta sank her hands into her pockets and made herself comfortable in one of the wicker chairs without responding. Or if she had, it was done in an elusive manner.

"I want to go to Chez Capoulade tonight" was all she offered. "If you want to join me, fine. If not, I'll go alone."

Her friend's expression grew serious. Her eyes appeared to be busy forming opinions, jumping to their own conclusions. She knew Gerta all too well.

"Are you sure?"

"Yes."

That could mean a number of things, thought Ruth. And one of them meant going back to the beginning. Winding up in the same place they thought they had escaped. But she kept quiet. She understood Gerta. How could she not? If she herself wanted to curl up and die each time she was at the Center for Refugees' section 4, where she worked, and was obliged to turn the newly arrived away, to other neighborhoods, where it was known that they'd also be rejected because there was no longer a way to offer shelter and food to everyone? The largest flood of refugees had arrived at the worst moment, just as unemployment was at its highest. The majority of the French believed they'd take the bread right out of their mouths; that's why there were more anti-Semitic protests in the streets. It was a bandwagon that had started in Germany and that was dangerously spreading everywhere.

Most of the refugees had to pass around the same 1,000-franc bill to present to the French customs authorities to prove their income and be granted entrance permission. But Gerta and Ruth were never as defenseless. Both were young and attractive, they had friends, spoke languages, and they knew what to do in order to get by.

"What you need is a real easygoing guy," said Ruth, lighting a cigarette and making it clear she wanted to change the subject. "Maybe that way you'll be less likely to complicate your life. Face it, Gerta, you don't know how to be alone. You come up with the most absurd ideas."

"I'm not alone. I have Georg."

"Georg is too far away."

Ruth directed her gaze at Gerta again, and this time with a look of disapproval. She always wound up playing the nurse, not because she was a few years older but because that's how things had always been between them. It worried Ruth that Gerta would get into trouble again, and she tried her best to help Gerta avoid it, unaware that sometimes destiny switches the cards on you so that while you're busy escaping the dog, you find yourself facing the wolf. The unexpected always arrives without any signs announcing it, in a casual manner, the same way it could simply choose to never arrive. Like a first date or a letter. They all eventually arrive. Even death arrives, but with this, you have to know how to wait.

"Today, I met a semi-crazy Hungarian," Ruth added with a complicit wink. "He wants to photograph me. He said he needs a blonde for an advertisement series he's working on. Imagine, some Swiss life insurance company . . ." she said, and then her face lit up with a smile that was part mocking, part mild vanity.

The reality was, anyone could have imagined her in one of those ads. Her face was the picture of health, rosy and framed by a blond bob parted to the left, with a patch of waves over her forehead that gave her the air of a film actress. Next to her, Gerta was undeniably a strange beauty with her gamin haircut, her severe cheekbones and slightly malicious eyes with flecks of green and yellow.

Now the two were laughing out loud, slouching in their wicker chairs. That's what Gerta liked most about her friend: the ability to always find the funny side to things, take her out of the darkest corners of her mind.

"How much is he going to pay you?" she asked in all pragmatism, never forgetting that however appealing the idea was to them, they were still trying to survive. And it wasn't the first time that modeling had paid a few days' rent or at least a meal out, for them.

Ruth shook her head, as if she truly felt bad dashing her friend's hopes like that.

"He's one of us," she said. "A Jew from Budapest. He doesn't have a franc."

"Too bad!" Gerta said, deliberately smacking her lips in a theatrical manner. "Is he at least handsome then?" she mused.

She had gone back to being the happy and frivolous girl from the tennis club in Waldau. But it was only a distant reflex. Or maybe not. Perhaps there were two women trapped inside her. The Jewish adolescent who wanted to be Greta Garbo, who adored etiquette, expensive dresses, and the classic poems she knew by heart. And the activist, tough, who dreamed of changing the world. Greta or Gerta. That very night, the latter was going to gain territory.

Chez Capoulade was located in a windowless basement on 63 Boulevard Saint-Michel. For months, leftist militants from all over Europe had started gathering there. Many of them were German and a few were from the Leipzig group, like Willi Chardack. The place was dimly lit, no brighter than a cave, and at the last minute everyone would show up: the impatient ones, the hard-core ones, the severe ones, those in favor of direct action, the ones that could be trusted. Impassioned looks, irritated gestures, lowering their voices to say that André Breton had joined the Communist Party, or to quote an editorial in *Pravda*, smoking cigarette after cigarette, like young privateers, quoting Marx, others Trotsky, in a strange dialect of concepts and retractions, theories and controversies. Gerta didn't participate in the ideological discussion. She kept herself at a distance, focused within herself. Not able to grasp it all. She was there because she was Jewish and anti-Fascist, and perhaps because of a sense of pride that didn't fit well within that language of axioms, quotes, anathemas, and dialectical and historical materialism. Her head was busy with other words, ones she heard that very morning near the Austerlitz station. Words that she was able to erase from her head for a while but that would return, with the grating sound of a handsaw, when she least expected.

"Je te connais, je sais qui tu es."

Chapter Three

Deep in thought, she walked behind them without a single misstep. Ruth had insisted she join them, leaving her with no other choice. The filtered light beneath the trees in the Luxembourg Garden made it feel as though they were passing through a huge crystal dome; it was one of literature's most frequented walks. Out of nowhere, Ruth ran beneath a horse-chestnut. Wearing a maroon-colored coat, she rested her back up against its trunk and smiled. Click. She had a talent for posing. From an angle, her face resembled one you would see in classic art. The sky cropped above her head like the jaw of an antelope. Click. With her coat collar lifted, she took three steps forward and then back, making a funny face to the camera, her head tilted to one side. Click. Without batting an eye, she passed right by the statues of the great masters: Flaubert, Baudelaire, Verlaine . . . bowing her head slightly when she came upon the bust of Chopin. Click. The sunlight scattered itself, like in a painting, over the tallest branches. Along the central path, her footsteps crunched over the gravel. The French were always so concerned with rationalizing spaces, putting up iron gates on the countryside. She ran her fingers over the surface of the pond and playfully splashed the photographer. Click.

Gerta observed and remained silent, as if this had nothing to do with her. Ultimately, she had gone only because her friend didn't fully trust the Hungarian. Although there was something about the spectacle that fascinated her. She had never been interested in photography, but to predict the invisible selection process of the mind when framing a shot seemed to her an exercise in absolute precision. Just like hunting.

The camera was light and compact, a high-speed 35-mm Leica with a focal-plane shutter.

"I just rescued her from a pawnshop."

The Hungarian excused himself, smiling, a cigarette hanging from the corner of his mouth. His name, André Friedmann. Black eyes, very black, like a cocker spaniel's, a small, moon-shaped scar over his left brow, a turtleneck, a film actor's good looks, upper lip slightly curled in an expression of disdain.

"She's my girlfriend," he joked, caressing the camera. "I can't live without her."

He had come with a Polish friend of his, David Seymour, who was also a photographer and Jewish. They called him Chim. He was thin and wore the glasses of an intellectual. It appeared as if they'd been friends a long time; both the kind who come off as uncouth, who place their glass on the table and never turn away anything that comes their way. Theirs was a friendship like Gerta and Ruth's, to some degree, although different. It's always different with men.

As they strolled around the Latin Quarter, they all took turns telling their stories, where they came from, how they ended up there, their refugee adventures . . . There was also the decorative part: Paris, September, the tall trees, the time that passes quickly when you are young or far away, or, better yet, when you're next to the Rue du Cherche-Midi, the sound of an accordion rising like a red fish over the pavement . . . By then Gerta had enough time to study the situation up close. Walking alongside André as if this was the natural order of things. They kept each other's pace, without tripping or getting in the way, though keeping their distance. Gerta took her time smoking and talking, without looking at him directly, focused solely on her analysis. She found him to be a bit conceited, handsome, ambitious, and like anyone, overly predictable at times. Seductive, without a doubt; also a tad vulgar, rough around the edges, and lacking in manners. That's when, while crossing Canal Saint-Martin, his hand reached under her blouse to touch her waist in an invasive manner. It didn't last more than a tenth of a second, but it was enough. Pure phosphorus. Gerta was immediately put on guard. But who the hell did this Hungarian think he was? She was brusque in her approach, looking as if she were about to say something unpleasant, her pupils radiant with green embers of rage. André just smiled a little, in a way that was simultaneously sincere and helpless. Almost shy. Like a child who has been wrongly accused. There was something in his eyes, a look of uncertainty, and it imbued him with charm. His desire to please became so evident that Gerta felt a vulnerability inside of her, like when she had been scolded as a child for something she hadn't done and sat on the porch steps fighting back the tears. Careful, she thought. Careful. Careful.

At least the photo session was informative. André and Chim discussed photography like members of a secret sect. A new esoteric sect of Judaism, whose course of action could extend from a meeting with Trotsky in Copenhagen to a European tour with the North American comedians Laurel and Hardy, whom André had recently photographed. To Gerta, it seemed an interesting way to earn a living.

"Not really," he said, disillusioning her. "There's a lot of competition. Half of the refugees in Paris are photographers or aspiring to be."

He spoke about inks for printing, movies in 35 mm, diaphragm apertures, manual dryers and tumble dryers, as if they were the keys to a whole new universe. Gerta listened, taking it all in. She was happy learning something new.

The day extended itself through plazas and into cafés. It was the perfect moment, when the words have yet to mean so much and everything transpires with levity; like André's mannerism of cupping his fingers to protect the flame for his cigarette. Hands that were tanned and confident. Gerta's way of walking, looking at the ground and veering a little to the left as if she was giving him the opportunity to occupy that space, smiling. Ruth was also smiling, though her smile was different, tinged with fatalism and resignation due to her friend's leading role, as if she were thinking, *Go with Little Miss Innocent.* But she wasn't serious. Just a little game of female rivalry. She walked behind them, offering the Pole some of her conversation because that was the part she'd been given to play that evening and she gave it her best. Today for you. Tomorrow for me. Chim just let her talk, somewhere between fascination and condescension. Watching her from a distance, the way certain men will look at women they consider out of reach. Each of them in their own way felt the effects of the moon that had peeked out into a corner of the sky that night. Bright, luminous, like a life full of possibilities still waiting to be revealed. Of mathematical probabilities and uncertain beginnings. Somewhere out there, in some roundabout of the night, colorful Chinese lanterns, music from a phonograph . . . The four of them dined in a restaurant André had recommended that had small tables with red-and-white checkered tablecloths. They ordered the most economical menu option, which consisted of rye bread, cheeses, and white wine. Chim pointed to a busy table in the back of the place, where the conversation revolved around a tall man wearing a wool hat with some kind of miner's light attached to it.

"It's Man Ray," he said. "He's always surrounded by writers. The man beside him with the tie and hatchet face is named James Joyce. A strange character. Irish. But he's worth listening to when he's very drunk."

Afterward, Chim pushed his glasses up the bridge of his nose with his index finger and fell into silence again. He didn't speak much, but when he did, whether induced by alcohol or not, he spoke about personal things, in a low voice, as if directed at his shirt collar. Gerta felt an immediate sympathy for him. He was shy and cultured, like an erudite Talmudist.

On the phonograph, Josephine Baker sang *"J'ai deux amours,"* which made Gerta think of avenues, narrow and black, like eels. Murmurs of conversation undulated all around, clouds of cigarette smoke, the perfect ambiance for sharing intimate feelings.

André carried the weight of the conversation. He'd let his words fall like someone who was out to narrow the gap. He spoke with vehemence, sure of himself, pausing every now and then to take a drag of his cigarette before starting up again. They'd been in Paris for more than a year, he said, trying to make their way, surviving on advertising assignments and sporadic work. Chim worked for *Regard*, the Communist Party's magazine, and lived on the specific assignments he was given by different agencies. It was important to have friends. And André had them. He knew people in the Agence Centrale and at the Anglo-Continental—the Hungarian diaspora, like Hug Block, who was a real handful, but he could rely on the Hungarians. He told jokes, smiled, said whatever popped into his head. Sometimes he'd look to see what was going on in the back of the place. Then turn back and fix his eyes on Gerta again. It was as if, with all of this, he was trying to say, these are my credentials. Keeping her chin down and eyes looking up, she listened with reflective thoughts of her own as he spoke. The expression on her face wasn't offering any easy promises, either. There was something punishing in it, with a fixed penetration, as if she were comparing or trying to distinguish what she had heard from what she was now hearing, perhaps venturing into judgments that weren't the kindest. To André, they were surprisingly light eyes, the color of olive oil, streaked with green and violet, like those flowers in the Budapest gardens of his childhood. He continued talking with confidence. Sometimes someone from l'Association des Écrivains et Artistes Révolutionnaires would send him a wire. Refugee solidarity. One of those gatherings hosted by the association was precisely how he met Henri Cartier-Bresson, a tall and aristocratic Norman, slightly surrealist, with whom he began developing photographs in his apartment's bidet.

"If they label you as a surrealist photographer, it's over," said André. His French was terrible, but he made an effort. "Nobody will offer you work. You become a real hothouse flower. But if you say you're a press photographer, the world is yours."

He didn't need to be asked direct questions to tell you his life. He was extroverted, a chatterbox, effusive. To Gerta he appeared too young. She estimated he was twenty-four or twenty-five years old. In reality, he had just turned twenty and still displayed a certain naïveté that boys can have when they pretend to be heroes. He exaggerated and embellished his own exploits. But he had charisma; when he spoke, all there was room for was to listen. Like when he told the story about the rebellion against Daladier's government. February 6, a rainy day. The Fascists had announced a colossal demonstration in front of the Palais Bourbon, and, in response, the Left organized several counterprotests of their own. It resulted in a pitched battle.

"I was able to get to Cours-la-Reine in Hug's car and afterward continued on foot to the Place de la Concorde, trying to cross the bridge to the Assemblée Nationale." André had begun to speak German, in which he was much more fluent. He was leaning on the edge of the table, his arms crossed. "There were more than two hundred policemen on horseback, six vans and police cordons in columns of five. It was impossible to cross. The people began surrounding a bus filled with passengers and that's where it all began: the fire, the stone-throwing, the broken glass, a head-to-head between Fascists from the Action Française and the Jeunesses Patriotes, against us. It only worsened throughout the night. None of the streetlamps worked. The only visible light came from torches and the bonfires people began creating." He brought his cigarette to his lips and looked straight at Gerta. He spoke with passion but with something else as well: vanity, habit, male pride. It's something that gets into men's heads and makes them behave like boys, right out of a scene from a western.

"It was raining and there was smoke everywhere. We knew that the Bonapartists had been able to get close to the Palais Bourbon, so we regrouped in an attempt to try and block them. But the police opened fire from the bridge. Several snipers had taken post up in the horse-chestnuts of Cours-la-Reine. It was a bloodbath: seventeen dead and more than a thousand wounded," he said, blowing out a fast stream of cigarette smoke. "And the worst part of it all," he added, "was not being able to take one damn photograph. There wasn't enough light."

Gerta continued looking at him closely, elbow at the edge of the table, chin resting in hand. Werner Thalheim had been detained that day and they ended up sending him back to Berlin, like many other comrades. The Socialists and the Communists kept brawling it out in their war of allegiances. André's friend Willi Chardack wound up with a broken collarbone and his head cut open. All the Left Bank cafés were converted into makeshift infirmaries . . . but this presumptuous Hungarian considered the fact that he couldn't take his goddamn photograph the biggest tragedy of all. Right.

Chim watched her with eyes that appeared smaller due to the thickness of his lenses, and she knew that in that very moment he was watching her think, and that perhaps he didn't agree with her, as if behind his pupils there lived the conviction that no one has the right to judge another. What did she really know about André? Had she ever been inside his head? Had they gone to school together? Did she ever sit beside him on the back steps of his house, petting the cat until sunrise, in order not to hear his family fight because his father had thrown away an entire month's salary in a card game? No, Gerta evidently did not know anything about his life or about Pest's working-class neighborhoods. How was she to know? When André was seventeen years old, two corpulent individuals in derby hats went and fetched him from his home after a series of disturbances by the Lánc Bridge. At police headquarters, the commissioner, Peter Heim, broke the boy's four ribs, never pausing to interrupt his whistling of Beethoven's *Fifth Symphony* throughout. His first swing went straight for the jaw, and André gave it to him with his cynical smile. The commissioner retaliated with a kick to the balls. This time, the boy didn't smile but gave him the dirtiest look he could muster. The beating continued until he lost consciousness. He remained in a coma for several days. After two weeks, he was let go. His mother, Júlia, bought him two shirts, a jacket, a pair of mountain boots with double soles, and two pairs of baggy pants, his refugee uniform. And put him on a train when he was just seventeen. He never had a home again. What did she know about all that had happened? Chim's eyes appeared to be asking this, as he scrutinized her reactions from behind his rounded glasses.

It was hard to imagine two teenagers less likely to wind up being friends than Chim and André. But despite the fact, they orbited one another like two celestial bodies floating through the air. They're so different, thought Gerta. Chim spoke perfect French. He seemed serious. Like a philosopher or a chess player. From the few comments he had made, Gerta was able to deduce that he was a staunch atheist, though he still carried his Jewish karma inside like a strand of sadness, as did she. André, in contrast, did not seem interested in complicating his life with such things. It appeared he complicated his in a different way, just as men always have. It all started because of a tall man with a mustache, who began speaking to Ruth in a tone that wasn't rude but suave. It had a certain gallantry to it, but with a good dose of alcohol. Nothing that a woman couldn't handle on her own, without making a scene but with a simple answer that

would put the Frenchy in his place. But before Ruth had time to respond, André was already getting up and throwing his chair behind
him with such force that everyone in the place stopped to look. His
hands slightly separated from his body, his muscles tensed.

"Easy," said Chim, getting up and removing his glasses just in
case they had to break open someone's face.

Luckily, it wasn't necessary. The guy, somewhat elusive and
resigned, simply put up his left hand as a form of apology. An edu-
cated Frenchman, after all. Or not looking for trouble that night.

It became apparent to Gerta, however, that this was not the
first time something like this had happened to them. Just from having watched him, she was certain that on more than one occasion
the situation had been resolved differently. There are men who are
born with an innate need to fight. It's not likely something that they
choose, but an instinct that causes them to jump at the first sign.
The Hungarian was one of them, righteous, accustomed to display-
ing the classic weaponry of a knight errant with women. And with
a dangerous inclination to engage in duels just before the last drink
of the night.

Despite this, when it came to both his life and work, he was,
or tried to appear, versatile and frivolous when he was lucid. He
had a peculiar sense of humor. Finding it relatively easy to laugh at
himself and his blunders, like when he spent in one afternoon the
entire advance that the Agence Centrale had given him and had to
pawn a Plaubel camera to pay the hotel. Or when he destroyed a
Leica trying to use it beneath the clear waters of the Mediterranean
while on assignment in Saint-Tropez for the Steinitz Brothers. The
agency went bankrupt a few months later, and André joked that it
was because they had hired him with his long list of disasters. His
carefree way of making fun of his own stupidities made him easygoing and likable on a first impression. Typical Hungarian humor.
His lazy smile expressed all that was needed, and he could even be
cynical without trying too hard. Above all, the way he would shrug

his shoulders, as if it made no difference whether he was photographing a war hero from the Bolshevik revolution or shooting a spread about chic vacation spots in the Riviera. Curiously, Gerta did not completely dislike such a duality. In some ways, she also enjoyed expensive perfumes and moonlit nights with champagne.

She couldn't say then what it was that didn't convince her about the Hungarian that eyed her so probingly, one hand holding his elbow, with a cigarette between two fingers. Without a doubt, there was something.

André Friedmann seemed to always land on his feet, like a cat. Only he could sink so deep and still maintain his boss's confidence; or travel on a German train with a passport and no visa, casually show the inspector an ornate bill from a restaurant instead of proper documentation, and actually get away with it. One of the two: either he was very clever or he had a gift for tipping the balance in his favor. As she studied them closer, neither of the two was especially reassuring, in Gerta's eyes.

"You know what being lucky is?" he asked, looking her straight in the face. "It's being at a bar in Berlin just as a Nazi SS officer begins to smash a Jewish cobbler's face, and not being the cobbler but the photographer who was able to take out his camera in time. Luck is something stuck to the bottoms of your shoes. You either have it or you don't."

Gerta thought about her star. I have it, she thought. But she kept it to herself.

André brushed the hair off his forehead and looked toward the back of the place again, at nothing in particular, momentarily in a daze. Sometimes he stared off into the distance, as if he were somewhere else. We all miss something, a house, the street that we played on as kids, an old pair of skis, the boots we wore to school, the book we learned to read with, the voice yelling at us from the kitchen to finish our milk, the sewing room at the back of the house, the clatter of the pedals. Homelands don't exist. It's an invention.

What does exist is that place where we were once happy. Gerta realized that André liked to return there sometimes. He'd be talking to everyone, boasting about something, smiling, smoking, when suddenly, out of nowhere, he'd get that look in his eye, and he was far away. Very far.

"Watch, you'll wind up sleeping with him," Ruth predicted when they finally arrived at their doorstep at dawn.

"Not for all the money in the world," she said.

Chapter Four

Any life, as brief as it may appear, contains plenty of misconceptions, situations that are difficult to explain, arrows that get lost in the clouds like phantom planes, and if it's out of sight, it's out of mind. It isn't easy piecing together all that information. Even if it's only for your own ears to hear. That's what the psychoanalysts were doing with their dream studies. Quicksand, winding staircases, melting pocket watches, and things like that. But Gerta's dreams were difficult to grasp or to try and frame. They were hers. What had her childhood been like up until then? A betrayal of those around her or else dreaming of another life?

She had found a modest paying job as a part-time secretary in the office of the émigré doctor René Spitz, a disciple of Freud. The majority of the pages in the early editions of his journals were filled with articles on dream interpretation. It was a world that wasn't completely foreign to Gerta. When work was slow, she would avidly read all the case studies, as if wanting to uncover a secret about her own life.

Everyone tries to manage their dreams in their own way. Sometimes, when she returned home, she would sit on her bed with an old box of quince candy that she used to store her treasures in: a pair of Egyptian amber earrings, photographs, a silver medallion with the silhouette of a ship, a pen drawing of the port in Ephesus that Georg had given her their last summer together. She suddenly felt the need to grasp at those memories like straws, as if they could protect her from something. From someone. She returned to the world of Georg as one shields oneself with armor. Constantly repeating his name. She forced herself to write to him as much as she could. Made plans to go see him in Italy. Something had stirred itself up inside, irritated her, left her disconcerted, and she sought refuge in an old lover. This was her limbo, trapped somewhere between reality and fiction. Why? Ruth studied her behavior while keeping her thoughts to herself. Recognizing the same defense mechanisms she'd seen her use as a girl.

One morning, when Gerta was nine and a student at the Queen Charlotte School, her teacher punished her by not allowing her to go and play outside. She pretended that she didn't care, as if she had always disliked having to go outdoors anyway. When Frau Hellen announced that her punishment was over, she stood her ground. For an entire year she remained indoors, reading alone at her desk, not wanting to grant the teacher the satisfaction of believing she had wounded Gerta. It wasn't that she was proud, just different. She never dealt well with being Jewish. Inventing stories about where she came from, like Moses saved from the water, or that she was the daughter of Norwegian whalers or pirates or, based on the novel she was reading, that her brothers formed part of King Arthur's Round Table, or that she had a star . . .

But there were other sorts of dreams, of course there were. There was the lake, the table covered in linen, a vase with tulips, John Reed's book, and a pistol. That was a whole other story.

Once, as she was leaving the doctor's office, she sensed someone walking behind her, but when she turned around to look, there was no one there, just a bunch of trees and streets. She kept walking from the Porte d'Orleans, through that area of vacant lands, and past Boulevard Jourdan, with a feeling of uneasiness at her back, as if she could hear a light squeaking of rubber soles. Every now and again a gust of wind would come, rustling up the papers and leaves, almost taking her and her scant 110 pounds with it as well. Bundled up in her coat and gray beret, she walked, eyeing the windows of the closed storefronts, seeing no one's reflection but her own. October and its shadows of longing.

She was thin, mostly due to fatigue. She slept poorly, burdened by a flood of blurry memories. It seemed centuries had passed since she abandoned Leipzig, yet she still hadn't found her place in this city.

"I know that one day I arrived in Paris," she would tell René Spitz in his office one afternoon when she decided to change her medical coat for the couch. "I know that for a while I lived at other people's expense, doing what others did, thinking what others thought." It was true. The reoccurring feeling that bothered her most was living a life that wasn't hers. But which was hers? She'd look at herself apprehensively in the bathroom mirror, staring at each of her features, as if at any given moment she could undergo a transformation with the fear that she'd no longer recognize herself. Until one day the change happened. She grabbed onto the sink with both hands, stuck her head beneath the faucet for a few minutes, and then shook her head to the sides like a dog in the rain. Afterward, she returned to studying herself in the mirror. Then, with the utmost care, she covered her hair, strand by strand, with red henna clay, using her fingers to comb it all back. She liked the color of dried blood.

"You look like a raccoon," Ruth said when she came home and found Gerta underneath a pile of blankets. Her red hair made her face appear harder and thinner.

Inside her house, she never hesitated to display who she really was. But outside, at the café gatherings, she became someone else. Dividing yourself in two, that was the first rule of survival: knowing how to differentiate exterior life from interior suffering. It was something she learned to do from an early age, in the same manner she learned how to express herself well in German at school and go home afterward and speak in Yiddish. By the end of the day, all curled up in her pajamas with a book, Gerta was nothing more than a pilgrim before the walls of a foreign city. On the outside, no less, she continued being the smiling princess with green eyes and flared pants, who had managed to dazzle the entire Left Bank.

Paris was one big party. With a simple bike wheel, wine rack, and a urinal, the Dadaists were capable of converting any night into an improvised spectacle. There was smoking, an ever-increasing amount of drinking, vodka, absinthe, champagne . . . Every day a manifesto was signed. In favor of popular art, by the Araucanian Indians, from the cabinet of Dr. Caligari, of Japanese trees . . . That's how they passed the time. The texts written one day were compared to ones written on others. The Paris carousel and Gerta giving it a whirl, turning on herself. She signed manifestos, assisted political meetings, read *Man's Fate* by Malraux, bought a ticket for a trip to Italy she never took, drank far too much some nights, and, above all, saw him again. Him. André. She even dreamed of him. Though it was more of a nightmare. He pressed down on her chest, completely aroused, making it impossible for her to breathe. She woke up screaming, with a frightened look in her eyes, staring straight at the pillow. Not wanting to move or rest her head on the same part of the bed. Perhaps that dream happened later on, who knows . . . It's also not that important. The fact was, she saw him again.

Of course, there's always chance. As well as destiny. There are parties, mutual friends who are photographers, electricians, or awful poets. Besides, everyone knows how small the world is, and that in one of its corners you can fit a terrace-balcony, from which you can see the Seine, hear the voice of Josephine Baker, like a long, dark street, and on which, just as she was heading back inside, the Hungarian grabbed her by the arm to ask her:

"Is it you?"

"Well," she responded in a dubious fashion, "not always."

The two share a laugh as if they've known each other for ages.

"I didn't recognize you," said André. Looking both shocked and amused, with a slight wink of the left eye, as if at any moment he would lunge like a hunter over its captive. "This bright red looks good on you."

"Perhaps," she said, readjusting her elbows on the balcony railing. She was going to say something about the Seine, about how beautiful the river looked with the moon looming over it, when she heard him say:

"It's not surprising that on nights like these people leap from bridges."

"What?"

"Oh nothing, it's just some verse," he said.

"No, really, I didn't hear you because of the music."

"That sometimes I want to kill myself, Red. Get it?" He said it loud and clear this time. Taking her chin in his hand and looking her straight in the eyes, never erasing that slightly sarcastic smile from his face.

"Yes, this time I heard you, and you don't have to yell," she said, taking the glass from his hand without his noticing. She hadn't realized until then that he was completely drunk.

A short time after, they were alone, walking along the riverbank, she letting him do the talking, half of her paying attention, the other half pitying him, as if he had come down with a fever or some harmless sickness that would soon pass.

What he had, which might very well pass or not, could be called deception, wounded pride, a desire to be fussed over, exhaustion . . . He had just returned from an assignment for *Vu* magazine in Saarland.

"Sarre . . ." he said its name in French as if he were dreaming.

But Gerta understood what he was trying to say. In other words, the League of Nations, carbon, *bonjour*, *guten Tag* . . . and all of that. André had told her that he had been in Saarbrücken during the last week of September, where there were posters and banners with swastikas everywhere. They walked along the river's edge, staggering slightly, him more than her, gazing at the moon, her coat collar up, shielding her from the night fog. He had gone with a journalist friend named Gorta, who—he went on to say—with his hair long and straight like a Sioux, was more like a Dostoevsky character than a John Reed. Carbon-filled clouds in the shape of whirlwinds had snuck into all parts of the city. There are steady winds and variable winds. Ones that change direction with a force that can knock down both jockey and horse. Winds that suddenly reorient themselves, turning the hands of time counterclockwise. Winds that can blow for years. Winds of the past that live in the present.

André's speech wasn't very well put together. He jumped from one thing to another, without transitions, using awkward word-ing. But nonetheless, Gerta, for some reason, at least that night, could see through his words as if they were images: at the forefront, an image of a cyclist reading the lists the Nazis had posted on the streetlamps, workers drinking beer below an equilateral cross or passed out in the shade beside the trash containers, the filthy gray of the sky, Saarbrücken's main street filled with banners hanging from its balconies, crowds of people leaving factories, cafés, greeting one another with a *"Heil Hitler,"* their arm raised, their smile casual, innocent, as if saying "Merry Christmas."

There were still a few months left until the plebiscite's out-come would decide if the territory would join with France or be-come a part of Germany. But, judging from the photos, there wasn't a doubt. The entire carbon basin had been won over by Fascism. SARRE—WARNING—HIGH ALERT was how the report's headline read. The images and text credited to a special correspondent by the name of Gorta. André's name did not appear anywhere in the report. As if the photographs were not his.

"I don't exist," he said with hands in his coat pockets, shoulders slumped, though she spotted the vertical lines at the corners of his mouth hardening. "I'm nobody." Now he smiled bitterly. "Just a ghost with a camera. A ghost photographing other ghosts."

Perhaps it was right then and there that she decided to adopt that man abandoned at the edge of the Seine, with those cocker spaniel eyes. Soon after, they found themselves sitting on a wooden bench. Listening to the trees, the river. Gerta with her knees to her chest, hugging her legs. For certain women, there's great danger in having someone place a fairy godmother's wand in their hands. I'll save you, she thought. I can do it. It may cost me and you might not deserve it, but I'm going to save you. There isn't a more powerful sensation than this. Not love, piety, or desire. Though Gerta still hadn't learned this, she was too young. That's why, somewhere along the way, she rubbed his head with a gesture that was a cross between messing up his hair and taking his temperature.

"Don't worry," she said in a good fairy's voice, poking her chin over her sweater. "The only thing you need is a manager."

She smiled. Her teeth were small and bright, with a tiny gap separating the two front ones. It wasn't the smile of a full-fledged woman but of a young girl—better yet, a fearless boy. An adventurous smile, the kind you put on in front of your opponent during a game. Tilting her head slightly to one side, inquisitive, teasing, as the idea ran through her head like a mouse in the floorboards above.

"I'm going to be your manager."

Chapter Five

It was all a game at first. That shirt I like, that one I don't. While he went into a changing room at La Samaritaine department store, she would wait for him at the entrance of the dressing area outside. Lounging with blasé entitlement on some sort of a red velvet sofa with her legs crossed, swinging one foot back and forth, until she saw him step out transformed into a fashion figure. Then, with arched eyebrows, she'd mockingly look him up and down, make him take the bullfighter's lap of honor, scrunching her nose a bit before giving him her approval. In reality, he looked like a film star: clean-shaven, a white collared shirt and tie, polished shoes, an all-American hairdo. His eyes, on the other hand, were still that of a Gypsy. This could not be fixed.

She enjoyed the distance that he maintained around himself, a space that was necessary in order for each to occupy their place. He was never bothered by her reprimands or when she told him what to do. He began calling her "the boss." This pact filled them both with a curious energy, as if there were a signal floating between them in the air, meeting at Le Dôme Café without having planned it, or when he passed below her window whistling without a care in the world, or, by coincidence, they both happened to be trying out a new restaurant on the very same night. Although by then, they both knew that their casual meetings were not the least bit casual.

Operation Image Makeover had its immediate results. Gerta was right. Her mother's teachings had proven themselves once more. Being elegant will not only improve your living, it can also help you earn one. Part two of the Sarre report became André's rite of passage. An air of success begets success.

Ruth rushed up the stairs with the breakfast baguette in one hand and the new edition of *Vu* magazine in the other. SARRE, PART TWO, stated the headline. ITS RESIDENTS' OPINIONS AND WHO THEY WILL VOTE FOR. Gerta, still in pajamas, desperately waited for her in the stairwell, wearing thick socks, her eyes swollen from having just woken up. And though it was still very early, she could hardly contain herself. Pushing aside the teapot and cups, she cleared a space on the kitchen table in order to spread open the magazine as if it were a map of the world. A flashy headline, its words moving across the page in a diagonal, and the photos she had originally seen stuck to the bathroom tiles as contact sheets were now enlarged and well emphasized on the page. She inhaled the smell of fresh ink from the page, as she had with her Magic Markers when she was young. In black lettering, the photo credit read: ANDRÉ FRIEDMANN. Gerta smiled over her gray pajama top and instinctively raised her fist to the air as a sign of victory. Exactly like Joe Jacobs did when he raised Max Schmeling's winning glove before the flashing cameras. When it comes down to it, not all boxing matches are fought inside the ring.

She liked to think of it as just a temporary alliance, nothing more. A mutual aid society for Jewish refugees. Today for you. Tomorrow for me. Besides, thought Gerta, it was not as if she had nothing to gain from it. She also received something in return. It was comforting to think like this, as if not getting too involved made her feel better. They got into the habit of waking up early to walk through the neighborhood and catch the first cart deliveries of fruit and fish to the markets. Together they'd wander through the streets with all the spices, behind the church of Saint-Séverin. The ringing of the bells passing through them both as they strolled in the fresh morning air, already charged with the smell of carbon and hemp. Foreigners in a dream city. The sky changing from indigo to gold with a soft gleam of light in the east. They were a strange-looking pair: a dark-haired guy dressed in a sweater and a blazer, and a redhead in tennis shoes and a Leica hanging from her shoulder like the bow of Diana the Huntress. She didn't always carry an extra roll of film with her, because she didn't want to waste a single franc, but she learned fast. Each kept to their own part of the sidewalk, without brushing up against the other, maintaining their distance. A day with beautiful light, a cigarette . . . That's all it was. In just a few weeks, she learned how to use the Leica and develop film in the bathroom using a piece of red cellophane to cover the lamp. André taught her how to get close to the object in question.

"You have to be there," he'd say, "glued to your prey, lying in wait, in order to be able to shoot at the exact moment, not a second before, not a second after." Click.

As a result of the lessons, she became more cautious and aggressive. Though when it came time to finding the perfect composition for an image, she lacked determination. She would just stand there on some corner near Notre Dame, focusing in on an old man with a thick beard and astrakhan hat, seeing a fragment of his thin cheek in relation to the Gothic portal of the Last Judgment, and lower her camera. She could capture it all with her eyes, except when it came to the temporal. The gray cobblestoned streets and silvery skies were not of interest to her anymore. It was something else. Perhaps she started to realize that what she was holding in her hands was a weapon. The reason why those long walks began to increasingly become a place to escape oneself, her special way of peeking out into the world—still easily surprised, maybe a tad too contradictory. The way you look at things is also how you think about and confront life. More than anything, she wanted to learn and to change. It was the perfect opportunity to do so, the moment when everything was about to happen, in which life's course could still alter itself. Many months later, just before daybreak in another country, beneath the rattling of machine guns in minus-five-degree weather, she would remember that initial moment when happiness was going out to hunt and not killing the bird.

"Photography helps my mind wander," she wrote in her diary. "It's like when I lie down on the roof at night and look at the stars." It was one of her favorite things to do during their vacations in Galicia. She'd climb out of her bedroom window and up to the rooftop, position herself face-up, and carve a hole in the night sky with her eyes. Taking in the summer breeze, not thinking about anything, in the middle of complete darkness. "In Paris, there are no stars, but there are the cafés' red lanterns. They look like new constellations created by the universe. Yesterday, while sitting at an outside table at Le Dôme, I sat in on a passionate debate about the visual power of the image between Chim, André, and that skinny Norm who joins us occasionally. He's an interesting character, that Henri, well-educated, from a good family, but at times you sense that guilt that people from the upper class have, their conscience conflicted because of their family's origins, and who then try to excuse themselves by being the most Leftist person at the table. André always teases him, saying that Cartier-Bresson never answers the telephone before reading the editorial in *L'Humanité*. But it isn't true. Other than being quick-witted and déclassé, Henri likes to consider himself free. They argue whether a photograph should be a useful documentation or the product of an artistic quest. It seems to me that the three of them think alike, but with different wording. But I don't fully understand.

"When I walk around the neighborhood with André, I'll look up at a balcony and suddenly, there's the photo: a woman hanging out her clothes to dry. It's something that has life, the antithesis of smiling and posing. Enough with having to know where one should be looking. I'm learning. I like the Leica; it's small and doesn't weigh a thing. You can take up to thirty-six shots in a row without having to carry around a light stand with you everywhere. In the bathroom, we've set up a darkroom. I help André, writing the photo captions, typing in three languages, and every now and again I'm able to get an ad assignment for Alliance Photo. It's not much, but it allows me to practice and get to know the inside world of journalism. The scene is not encouraging. It's not easy to break through; you have to elbow your way in. At least André has good contacts. Ruth and I got a new job typing up handwritten screenplays for Max Ophüls. I'm also still working at René's office on Thursday afternoons. With all of this we have enough to pay the rent, though it barely lasts us until the end of the month. But at least I don't owe anyone money. Oh, and we have a new roommate, a parrot from Guiana, a present from André, with an orange-colored beak and a black tongue—poor thing arrived a bit beaten up. Ruth has resigned herself to teaching it French, but it still hasn't said a single word, prefers to whistle the "Turkish March." It can't fly, either, although he feels at liberty to move around the house bow-legged like an old pirate. They wrote his name for us, but we decided to call him Captain Flint. What else?

"Chim gave me a photo that his friend Stein took of me and André at the Café de Flore. I hardly recognize myself. I'm wearing my beret to the side and I'm smiling, looking down as if someone were telling me a secret. André is wearing a sporty jacket and a tie and appears to have just said something funny. Things have started going better for him, and he can afford fancier clothes, although he doesn't manage to put them together so well, you might say. He'll look right at me, trying to detect my reaction, smiling, or barely. We look as if we were lovers. That Stein will go far with his photography. He's good at waiting for the moment. He knows exactly when to press the shutter. Only we aren't lovers or anything close to the sort. I have a past. There's Georg. He writes me every week from San Gimignano. We're born with a mapped-out route. This one, not that one. Who you dream with. Who you love. It's one or the other. You choose without choosing. That's how it is. Each of us travels on their own path. Besides, how do you love someone without truly knowing who they are? How do you travel that distance when there's all that you don't know about the other?

"Sometimes I am tempted to tell André what happened in Leipzig. He also doesn't speak much about what he's left behind, though he's capable of talking for hours on end about anything else. I know that his mother's name is Júlia and that he has a little brother whom he adores tremendously, Cornell. There have only been a few occasions in which he opens a window onto his life for me to look through. He's extremely guarded. I, too, grow silent sometimes when I look back in time and see my father standing in the gymnasium's doorway in Stuttgart, waiting for me to tie my shoelaces, growing a bit impatient, glancing at his watch. Then I can hear Oskar and Karl in the stands, cheering me on: '*Go, Little Trout* . . .' It's been ages since someone has called me that. It's been ages since we went down to the river to throw stones. Cleaned the mud off our shoes with blades of grass. On nights like these, I wonder if it's as painful for them to be remembered as it is for me to remember them. They have had to escape several times from the Führer and his decrees. Now they're in Petrograd, with our grandparents, near the Romanian border. It's a small Serbian village that's never had an anti-Semitic tradition, and because of this, I worry less. I don't know if I'll ever be able to feel proud of being Jewish; I'd like to be more like André, who isn't affected by this in the least. To him, it's like being Canadian or Finnish. Never could I comprehend the Hebrew tradition of identifying with your ancestors: 'When we were expelled from Egypt . . .' Listen, I was never expelled from Egypt. For better or for worse, I can't carry that load with me. I don't believe in that kind of *we*. Organized groups are just a bunch of excuses. Only the action of an individual holds a moral meaning, at least in this life. Frankly, the other kind doesn't convince me. It's true that the beautiful parts we were taught as children exist. The story of Sarah, for example, or the angel who held on to Abraham's arm, the music, the Psalms . . .

"I remember that on Yom Kippur, the day where it's written that each man should forgive his neighbor, they dressed us in our best clothes. There was a photo on top of the bureau, of Karl and Oskar wearing baggy pants and new shirts. I was wearing a short dress with cherries all over it. Skinny legs. My hair was in a bun on top of my head, like a little gray cloud. Images are never forgotten. Photography's mystery."

Knock-knock . . . someone tapped lightly on the door. It had been a while since she last heard the pounding of the typewriter keys in the room next to hers. It must have been around one in the morning. When Ruth peeked in, she saw Gerta sitting with a notebook on her knees, all wrapped up in a blanket, with her third cigarette of insomnia hanging from the edge of her mouth.

"You're still awake?"

"I was about to go to sleep." Gerta apologized like a little girl caught doing something wrong.

"You shouldn't keep a diary," said Ruth, pointing to the red-covered notebook that Gerta had placed on top of her nightstand. "You never know into whose hands it may fall." She was right: this went completely against the basic norms of keeping a low profile.

"Right . . ."

"Then why do you do it?"

"Don't know," Gerta said, shrugging. Then she put out her cigarette in a small, chipped plate. "I'm afraid of forgetting who I am."

It was true. We all have a secret fear. A terror that's intimate, that's ours, differentiating us from the rest. A unique fear, precise.

Fear of not recognizing your own face in the mirror, of getting lost on a sleepless night in a foreign city after drinking several glasses of vodka. Fear of others, of being devastated by love or, worse, by loneliness. Fear as extreme consciousness of a reality that you only discover at a given moment, although it's always been there. Fear of remembering what you did or what you were capable of doing. Fear as an end to innocence, rupturing a state of grace. Fear of the lake house with the tulips, fear of swimming too far from the edge, fear of dark and viscous waters on your skin when there's no longer a trace of firm earth beneath your feet. Fear with a capital *F*. *F* as in *Fatal* or to *Finish Off*. Fear of the constant fog of autumn over those remote neighborhoods through which she has to pass on Thursdays, with its deserted plazas and scant faces, a beggar here, a woman pushing a cart full of wood over on the other corner. And the sounds of her own footsteps, their tone soft, quick, and moist . . . as if they weren't hers but those of someone following her from a distance, one, two, one, two . . . that relentless, threatening feeling you carry with you in your neck all the way home, beret tightly in place, hands in pockets, that pressing need to run. Like when she was a little girl and had to cross the alleyway from the bakery to Jakob's house, holding her breath as she climbed the stairs, two by two, until she rang the doorbell and the light went on, and she was in safe haven. Easy, she'd say to herself while trying to slow down her pace. Take it easy. If she stood still for a moment, the echo would stop, if she started up again, the rhythm would pick up again, repeating itself: one, two, one, two, one, two, one two . . . Once in a while she turned her head to look and there was nothing. Nothing. Maybe it was all in her head.

Chapter Six

She sat for a while, contemplating the page she finished typing. Engrossed in it, unaware of its content but conscious of the porosity of the paper, the impression each character had left. Black ink. Alongside the typewriter, there was a stack of handwritten pages with green blotting paper between them. Gerta twisted the roller, removed the sheet, and began reading it closely: "In the face of Nazism spreading itself throughout Europe, we are left with only one solution: uniting Communists, Socialists, Republicans, and other Leftist parties, into one anti-Fascist coalition that will facilitate the formation of wide-ranging political groupings (. . .). The alliance of all democratic forces into one Popular Front."

"What do you think, Captain Flint?" she said, looking up at the shelf where they set up the trapeze for the bird to do its stunts. Since André had left for Spain, she found herself talking more to the parrot. Another of her tactics for combating loneliness. Just like her return to being her old militant self. She felt the urgent need to help, be useful, serve a purpose. But in what? Not a clue. She tried to find out by going back to the gatherings at Chez Capoulade, which had only grown more popular with time. Woman-echo, Woman-reflection, Woman-mirror. Inside, there was always too much cigarette smoke. Too much noise. Gerta grabbed her glass of vodka, still half-full, and went outside to sit on the edge of the sidewalk and smoke a cigarette. She sat there, hugging her knees, looking up at the patchy sky, a star here, another there, between eave and eave, with a faint orange glow toward the west. She felt good like this, breathing in the aroma of lime trees during spring's recent debut. The silence of that city appealed to her, with its labyrinth of stoned promenades creeping down to the river. That calm brought her peace. It allowed her to organize her thoughts. She remained like this awhile, until someone placed their hand on her shoulder. It was Erwin Ackerknecht, her old friend from Leipzig.

"We need someone to type the text to the manifesto in French, English, and German," he said, taking a seat next to her on the pavement. "The more intellectuals we can gather the better. We have to make this congress a success." He was referring to the International Congress of Writers for the Defense of Culture, which was to be held in Paris in the early fall. Erwin took his time rolling a cigarette between his fingers, then wetting the paper with his lips to seal it. "Aldous Huxley and Forster have already confirmed their attendance," he added, "as well as Isaac Babel and Boris Pasternak from the USSR. Representing us will be Bertolt Brecht, Heinrich Mann, and Robert Musil, from Austria. The Americans still haven't confirmed . . . It's important that this document reaches everyone, Gerta, each one of them, in their own language. Can we count on you for this?"

"Of course," she said. She took a sip of her vodka drink, allowing the alcohol to find its way into her veins, passing through her heart and up to her brain. She found it tasted harsh, mixed with the tobacco. Brushing a patch of hair off her forehead, she looked out into the sky. Like just another sentry in the night, Saint-Germain-des-Prés' thousand-year-old abbey and its Romanesque bell tower stood tall, framed in black.

In recent weeks, the surrealists' controversies had shifted away from poetic boundaries to concentrate instead on the reality that was being reported in the media. Their desires grew dim, and the small group from the Left Bank temporarily abandoned the astral heights of Mount Olympus and muses with green-colored eyes, so they could take part in the world's grand whirlwind. While they awaited further news, a latent conflict persisted between those who accepted the revolutionary party's plans and those who still aspired to unite the revolution with poetry. It was not a trifling matter. Walking down the boulevard one afternoon, André Breton, on his way to buy tobacco at the shop next to Dôme, bumped into the Russian Stalinist Ilya Ehrenburg, just as the latter was leaving. Neither chose their words carefully. The poet took a deep breath and, on the same impulse, punched Ehrenburg in the nose with a crack that sounded as if a chair had broken. It wasn't a premeditated act. It simply happened. Caught by surprise, the Russian didn't have time to react. Weakened by the blow, he fell to his knees, dripping a scandalously red-colored blood over the gray pavement. Afterward, as if they were all possessed, it turned into a messy battle with everyone against everyone. There were insults; some people got up to help the wounded man, while others tried to calm the poet's fury. They tried to lift the Russian, get him out of there, until someone shouted something about calling the police, and in that moment they all decided to walk away from the boxing match between mastiffs until the next time. A few days later, René Crevel, the poet in charge of trying to make peace between the surrealists and the Communists, committed suicide in his kitchen by opening the gas valve.

"It's always necessary to say good-bye," he wrote, having lost hope. "Tomorrow, you will return to the fog of your origins. To a city, red and gray, your colorless room, its silver walls, and with windows that open directly onto the clouds to which you are sister. To search for the shadow of your face throughout the sky, the gestures of your fingers . . ."

That was the state of things when Gerta found herself obliged to choose between two options she didn't like. It was no secret how dissidents in the Soviet Union were repressed, but in that small Montparnasse community, the sacred dwelling of the gods, many were unsure whether to denounce Stalin's abuses or keep them quiet in order to preserve the unified band of anti-Fascists.

She thought for a while, as if floating over an abyss, with the manifesto in one hand and a cigarette in the other. She wasn't reading the words, just smoking and looking at the white fabric covering the sofa, and the shelf with the clay figurines that Ruth bought from a peddler. Despite all their efforts to convert that place into a home, it never stopped being a temporary camp: the taped-up glass on the kitchen doors, a map of Europe in the living room, the hallways lined with stacks of books on the floor, a small bottle with lilacs in the window, random photographs tacked onto the wall . . . André, with the sleeves of his blazer rolled up, waving good-bye from the Gare de l'Est. She missed him, of course she did. But it wasn't something irreparable; more like a gentle sensation untangling itself imperceptibly. Without a loud roar, but with a kind of familiarity. Nothing serious. She had opened up the window and propped her elbows on the windowsill when a breeze came her way, refreshing her skin and memory: mornings spent running around the neighborhood with the Leica; André's teachings, his way of installing himself in time without ever looking at a watch, as if it was up to everyone else to adapt to his rhythm; the day he arrived with Captain Flint on his shoulder; the false negligence with which he kept his developing liquids on the top shelf of the bathroom; his way of always showing up at the last minute with a bottle of wine under his coat and a basket of trout, fresh off the boat; the way he laughed while turning on the kitchen stove, while Chim spread out the tablecloth and Ruth removed the plates and glasses from the cupboard and arranged the silverware on the table in pure gala style. The quick carelessness in all his gestures. His arrogance at times, fused with a peculiar aptitude to be what he didn't seem to be and to appear as he wasn't. Behind which mask was he hiding? Which was he? The happy bohemian and seducer or the lonely man who could sometimes fall into silence on the other side of a collapsing bridge? "I'm nothing, nothing." Gerta remembered how he told her this near the edge of the Seine. He used his fragility to hide his pride. Perhaps all his charm was rooted in his ability to pretend: in the shyness he instinctively hid his courage within, his way of smiling, or shrugging his shoulders, as if nothing was wrong, when in reality he was furious. So many contradictions: his blazer hanging open, those strong hands, his worldly air, and that rare ingenuity of an obedient child when he allowed someone to counsel him on his wardrobe. But that costume game brought results. If it wasn't for that respectable new image that wearing a jacket and tie gave him, *Berliner Illustrierte Zeitung* magazine would never have given him that assignment he was now on in Spain. At first he was hesitant about accepting the offer, because the magazine, like all German publications, found itself part of Goebbels's iron-fisted propaganda machine. But he wasn't exactly in a position to be able to choose or reject his projects. All he was asked to do was interview the Basque boxer Paulino Uzcudun, scheduled to fight the German heavyweight champion Max Schmeling in an upcoming match in Berlin.

André's fascination with Spain was instantaneous. There were days when he returned to his *pensión*, and as big as he was, he'd throw himself on the bed listening to La Niña de Marchena or to Pepita Ramos, and it reminded him of home. The country reminded him a great deal of Hungary, those rowdy streets, the tavern scene with its strings of garlic hanging from the ceilings, wineskins filled with red wine, stages for flamenco . . . The Gypsy within him did not hold back. He joined right in, taking portraits of those around him with such a penetrating intensity it was as if he were trying to rob them of their souls. When he was finished with his sports assignment in San Sebastián, he continued onto Madrid to cover the huge protest on April 14, the fourth anniversary of the Republic's proclamation. There was a charge in the air, and André could feel the tension in the streets. How they hated the Confederación Española de Derechas Autónomas (CEDA), the right-wing coalition that, less than a year ago, government-led, had launched an attack on the miners rebellion in Asturias. The wounds were still fresh, but the political issue did not stop the Spaniards from celebrating their holidays and religious festivals as they wished. Sevilla's Holy Week, for instance, where André had arrived by train, along with a thousand other visitors, to soak up the imagery: women with mantillas and pinned carnations cheering on the passage of Jesús del Gran Poder, singing songs of devotion to all the passing brotherhoods, the Nazarenos dressed as Ku Klux Klan, zigzagging through the narrow streets and the firecracker smoke until dawn. He had never imagined a festival where the sacred and the profane were so intertwined. Observing it all objectively, with a look that still hadn't been fully adjusted, still a bit raw and superficial but forming a new layer of skin to it all: dancers in frilly dresses stomping furiously in the April wind, young men on horseback, Premier Alejandro Lerroux touring the city in a carriage whose horses were adorned *à la Andalucia*, fun-loving drunks, tourists, cats perched on undulating tin-plated rooftops. An old man in his doorway sharpening a knife, next to him a small bundle covered in cloth with an opening on one side revealing the dark-skinned little face of a sleeping Gypsy girl. The war was about to begin.

"You have to experience this country," he wrote Gerta in a letter, not knowing that in a short while she'd be traveling through it, under fire from antiaircraft weaponry, still alive within the dead lights of the cities. How strange life can be. But André couldn't have known this as he described his impressions of the trip in an awkward German, from the American Bar at the Hotel Cristina, with a three-day-old beard, shirtless, and moneyless, after having spent the entire night drinking. "Sometimes I wish you were here" was how he finished the letter.

That he tempted everyone around him was part of his charm, as was his lack of discipline, his way of appearing self-centered and slightly conceited. A touch of womanizer in him. This, Gerta could not ignore.

Sometimes . . . she repeated to herself, rereading the letter. What an imbecile.

Chapter Seven

She remained standing in front of her door for a while, house key in hand. The door's strike plate had been forced and little bits of wood were scattered on the floor. Before she had time to think, she noticed how the blood throbbed in her left temple, a vague, discomforting feeling similar to sensing footsteps behind her while walking home. Her entire body tensed up like an arc, the instinctive precaution of the hare who can smell its hunter. She had imagined this scenario so many times in her head that she no longer recognized it. It was seared into her memory the moment she first stepped foot into that jail cell in Wächterstrasse. There was a muffled pounding in her eardrums, consistent, like waves. She had experienced something similar at the lake, several meters below the water. When you swim under water, you can even hear the blood run through your veins, though not a single sound from the outside world can reach you. If someone were to have called her name in that moment, she would not have been able to hear them. Nor the sound of a gunshot, perhaps.

Instinctively, she held on to the camera bag resting over her stomach and opened the door slowly with her foot.

"Ruth?" she called out. "Are you there?"

As she entered the hallway, her imagination began registering the chain of events bit by bit: the broken lock, torn-up pieces of paper, a load of gutted books all over the hallway, the photographs torn from the wall, the little glass vase in smithereens, overturned drawers, a bead from her amber necklace rolling across the floor, those equilateral crosses painted on the wall. "Filthy Jews." The same old story . . . She detected a strange odor in the house. The sound of boiling water coming from the kitchen. A second before she uncovered the pot, she already knew what she'd find. Captain Flint floating on the surface with a broken neck and his tongue sticking out. She didn't scream. All she did was turn off the flame and close her eyes. A pang of shame and humiliation galloped up her throat, causing her to retch. She needed a cigarette and sat down on the floor to smoke it, her back against the wall under the swastika. Knees bent, her forehead in her hand. Suddenly it became clear that this was never going to end, that it would always be like this. Either black or white. Or this or that. Who you're with, in what you believe, who you hate. Who will kill you. In her head, she could hear the faint echo of a handsaw: "*Je te connais, je sais qui tu es.*"

All the metaphysical anguish she experienced during those gatherings at Chez Capoulade were now transformed into pure hate. Specific. Clear. It had nothing to do with ideology but rather with instinct, along with the need to break open somebody's head. To fight knowing precisely why you're fighting, to revive the reflexes, the basic elements of defense and self-preservation, tense the muscles, learn how to load and unload a weapon, improve your aim . . .

"It's either you or them, Little Trout." She recalled Karl's voice on the rooftop, trying to instruct her in case the moment should ever come.

The memory stirred up something inside. She missed her brothers. She noted a soft tickling on her side before the tears began clouding her vision.

Damn it, she said. Stupid damn Jew. Are you going to give those sons of bitches the satisfaction of bringing you to tears? She slammed the floor with her fist, brusquely, with a desperate rage aimed more at herself than anybody else, and on the same impulse she stood up, took the camera out of its bag—placing her eye on the viewfinder, adjusting the focus, then the diaphragm, first framing the parrot's limp head, closing in on its tongue—and began to shoot. Hardened look, her nostrils dilated, her hands steady, white knuckles each time she pressed the shutter. Click. Click. Click. Click. Click . . .

When Ruth and Chim arrived, they didn't need to ask what had happened. They found her leaning on the kitchen table, her shirtsleeves rolled up above her elbows, frowning, concentrated on gluing back together the books that could still be salvaged. She was pale and wore a tense expression, obstinate, disciplined, as if that manual task was the only thing that could help her control her emotions. She didn't move when they arrived or say a word. Chim weaved through the debris so he could hug her, but she put the brakes on him with her hand. She didn't need comforting from anyone.

"They take anything?" he asked.

"Nothing essential." Her voice sounded more gloomy than fragile. Her tennis shoes and clothes hanging in the back wardrobe were the only things that had survived the raid intact. "They boiled Captain Flint alive."

"You have to leave this house," Chim tried reasoning. "They can return at any time."

"And what good would that do?" said Gerta. "If they look, they'll find you. The only thing we can do is be prepared in case it happens again."

Ruth knew perfectly what she was referring to but preferred not to argue with her friend this time. "They didn't have to kill him," she said. "He was an old and amusing bird; he'd go with anyone."

Gerta turned her face to the wall so they wouldn't see her expression and swallowed saliva, but turned back soon after. While Chim tried convincing her, she remained motionless, her hand supporting her head. All his reasoning proved completely useless in making them desist. But they at least welcomed his offer to stay and sleep there that night. He would never think of leaving them alone.

With the frenetic passion of those who, in reality, are trying to change the world, they dedicated the rest of the day to repairing all the damages. They plugged up the holes in the lock with filler. Ruth packed the typewriter in a leather bag to bring to a friend's office in Le Marais. Chim was in charge of taking Captain Flint with him, wrapped up in a towel. Despite all her character and strength, Gerta did not have the heart to do it. He looked even smaller, like that, with his feathers drenched. Chim looked at him with affection, remembering his bow-legged walk, up to his old tricks all over the living room. He had never learned to talk, but on occasion he had the ability to listen with an intelligence that many humans would envy. Later, Chim climbed up a ladder with a brush in his hand and a hat made of newspaper on his head, absorbed in leaving the walls in the hallway immaculate, like pieces of eternity. His arms were speckled with tiny drops of paint. By the end of the day, everything seemed to be pretty close to being back in its place. You could say that the house had been able to withstand its first attack. Everything was impregnated with the smell of paint and solvent. They opened the windows and delighted in breathing in that uncertain air of summer's beginnings.

The political climate couldn't have been more heated. England's refusal to help France detain Hitler's remilitarization of the Rhineland caused the French to think they'd been abandoned by their main ally. The constant movement of Mussolini's troops on the border of Abyssinia didn't exactly help ease nerves, either. Rarely was there a Sunday in which Paris streets weren't filled with marching protesters. Hundreds of thousands of people regularly flocked to the streets with flags, banners, and dispatches that the formation of the Popular Front would soon be taking off. Chim, Henri Cartier-Bresson, Gerta, Fred Stein, Brassaï, André Kertész . . .

photographers from all over Europe captured the fervor, perched on cornices, from up in the trees or rooftops. Students, neighborhood workers from Saint-Denis, circles of people arguing heatedly in the Marais neighborhood . . . Something was about to happen. Something serious, important . . . and they wanted to be there to capture it with their cameras. Leica, Kodak, Linhof, Ermanox, Rolleiflex with the twin-lens reflex . . . lit up viewfinders, zoom, semiautomatics, filters, tripods . . . Carrying everything over their shoulders. They were nothing more than photographers, people dedicated to looking. Witnesses. And unaware that they were living between two world wars. A good majority were already used to clandestinely crossing borders. They were no longer German, or Hungarian, or Polish, or Czechoslovakian, or Austrian. They were refugees. They belonged to no one. Not to any nation. Nomads, stateless people who gathered almost every week somewhere to read aloud passages from novels, recite poetry, act out plays written by Bertolt Brecht against Nazism, or give conferences. A certain romanticism united them. Give me a photograph and I'll build you the world. Give me a camera and I'll show you the map of Europe, an ailing continent with all its contours under threat, emerging from the acid in the developing tray: the face of an old man at Notre Dame; a woman in mourning before a tombstone at the Jewish cemetery, her eyes closed, whispering a prayer; and just shortly afterward, a boy lifting his hands in the Warsaw ghetto; a soldier with his eyes bandaged, dictating a letter to his fellow soldier; dark silhouettes of buildings against a scene of flashing explosions in black-and-white; Gerta crouching in a trench coat with a camera hanging around her neck, a slightly distorted focus while framing a bridge in flames, the geometry of horror. It wouldn't be long before that world would go on to become one of the many scenes of war.

On Rue Lobineau, every second and last Saturday of the month, there was a small flea market of exotic merchandise, spices from India, perfumes in bottles of all different colors, indigo-colored fabrics, henna for the hair, tropical birds like Captain Flint. Every time she walked in front of that stand, she thought of him. She'd look at those birds with green- and orange-colored feathers, remembering the illustrations of a book she read as a girl, its turquoise cover featuring a pirate with a parrot on his shoulder.

Her imagination always played tricks on her. She had a narrative mind: Long John Silver, *Treasure Island*, and all of that. She was far too impressionable. Raised in a world that was on the brink of extinction, and the Captain Flint episode affecting her far more than she was willing to admit. Not only because of how much she cared for it, or the familiarity of seeing it walking around the house every day, but because what happened had been a senseless act. Absurd. Unnecessary savagery. However, the thought of replacing the old parrot from Guiana never occurred to her. She wasn't one of those. Not feeling the need to fill the holes being left empty in her heart. She walked through all the stalls, sucking in that chaotic tide of sensations. The smell of ginger and cinnamon, the cries of the vendors, the screech of the birds, capturing images as an explorer would in an unfamiliar world.

Chim had arranged for Fred Stein to stay in a free room they had in their flat. He was a quiet man, and timid, with an innate sense of photographic composition. The fact that he was German, and a refugee, helped sway their initial resistance to letting him stay with them. On the other hand, it didn't hurt to have someone else help them with the rent. After the incident with the Fascists from the Croix de Feu, they felt more secure with a man in the house, though they refused to admit it. Everyone suspected the leading anti-Semitic French groups were directly linked to Germany. And this wasn't at all comforting, especially considering Gerta's past.

Fred had a distinct approach to photography, offering a fresh perspective for capturing the pedestrian moment, less intuitive perhaps but more sensorial. When he photographed one of the birds with the bright and colorful plumage, one could immediately understand the sequence; how it had been captured in a tropical jungle, placed into a bamboo cage for countless days so it could enter the river of commerce, until it arrived at a stall on Rue Lobineau.

When it came time to frame her shots, Gerta also absorbed Fred's distinct point of view, one that was different from the perspective that André had taught her but complementary, to a certain degree. Less exact yet more evocative. The fact that logic didn't always work at the moment of truth was proven day after day in the news reports. She was trying to discover for herself what exactly she wanted to transmit in her photography. Her innocence hadn't been completely lost yet. Despite everything, she was still the girl who liked to throw herself down on the rooftop in Galicia, face-up, breathing in the clean air of the stars, floating within the darkness, the coolness of her back inside her pajama top. How strange it was to swim afterward, as a woman, touched by the cold fingers of the lake. She was an excellent swimmer; able to cross from one side of the lake to the other in record time. That's why they called her "Little Trout" at home.

Every night, just before going to sleep in her Paris bedroom, she crossed the border toward those memories and returned to being that ten-year-old girl in a photograph she kept. Standing on a dock in a red bathing suit, her back wet, the blond points of her braids, dripping like paint brushes, very skinny legs, birdlike, and always thinking about her star. She imagined it to be lime-green, the color of mint candy. She kept the memory in her mouth until it dissolved, little by little, within the fresh breath of her dream. The following morning, when she went out early to take photos in the neighborhood, her muscles could feel the cold water's concentrated energy in each stroke, as if she were swimming toward the future. Sometime after that, in the red half-light of her bathroom, while watching the lines and forms appear on the developing tray, she'd discover that the image can be deceiving. Just one false move, the slow configuration of a face, the foreshortening of a falling body, a shirt too clean for a soldier who has spent long hours struggling in combat. But those kinds of details and others, more or less evident, she still couldn't have known. She lacked the experience and depth of field, that scab of time that can age the gaze of a twentysomething-year-old woman in just a few hours.

Depth of field is something you can't foresee. It appears when it appears. Some are never able to capture it in a lifetime. Others are born with their days numbered, and they have to hurry to get it, in the short time they have left. Gerta was one of the latter, a long-distance runner. She rushed through her days like cigarettes, waiting for the moment. She stood still, leaning on the windowsill, wearing a black spaghetti-strapped shirt, the sun on the skin of her shoulders. June 24, 1935. Summer solstice. Noon. Not a breath of air. Suddenly she saw a square of light on the far end of the street and felt a tingling in her stomach. She focused with more precision: the white shirt, rolled-up sleeves, the wet hair, the equipment slung over the shoulder, skin tanned from the Spanish sun. The sensation was similar to when a ship jolts and the floor tilts beneath you. Her disorderly heartbeat caught her by surprise, but it was not the moment to stop and analyze her emotions. Nor did she even wait for him to come up. She ran downstairs, two steps at a time, and he lifted her in his arms. In the doorway, as her father always had when he returned home from a trip. Twirling her through the air, half-smiling, sure of himself, fraternal as always. André, and his way of always showing up when you least expect it, with those eyes that granted him forgiveness. So handsome it hurt, she thought. The Hungarian Jew.

Chapter Eight

Night was falling. The ocean dark. And up there, once again, the stars, dense as the calligraphy of an indecipherable manuscript. A soft breeze that smelled of pine and eucalyptus, almost imperceptible, grazed the water with a strange silvery phosphorescence. Gerta and André had been lying down on the sand for a while, face-up and without speaking. As if they were on a boat deck and looking out from the island toward the bright city of Cannes with its red and blue lights shining brightly on the horizon. They both had on the sweaters that Ruth suggested at the last minute they pack in their bags. "They will come in handy at night," she'd said. Gerta could smell the wool on André's sleeve as she rested her head on his arm.

It was a small and calm fishermen's island. Barely 370 acres of Mediterranean pines, with a few docked *feluccas*, nets placed out to dry, and the smell of old port. The perfect resting place for a warrior. André had returned from Spain tired and with a fresh batch of money from the report he sold to *Berliner Illustrierte*. The francs were burning holes in his pockets; he wasn't cut out for being rich. So, when he found out that Willi Chardack and some other people they knew were thinking of taking a trip to the Lérins Islands in the Côte d'Azur, he didn't think twice. He suggested that Chim and the girls come along. Although Ruth had thought it was a great idea, she couldn't go. She had just signed a contract with the film-maker Max Ophüls for a small part in a film called *Divine*, which had begun shooting in Paris. Chim had a deadline for an assignment he accepted from *Vu* magazine, about the Left Bank's artists, and decided to stay. André looked over at Gerta, standing there with her bony chin, a slight frown, as she thought it through.

"All right. Why not?" She smiled in agreement.

They made their way to Cannes hitchhiking. Both in an excellent mood, joking around, stealing fruit from orchards, dining at highway café-bars, leaving behind small villages that smelled of sweet broom. New horizons that whet your appetite and make you want to laugh hard, breathe in the fresh air, and get lost in the world. They were seized by a kind of euphoric vitality. Life's invisible paths. From Cannes' port, they took a small fishing boat to Île Sainte-Marguerite while the sun darted across the water. There is a strip between the ocean and the earth. Just as there's an ambiguous strip, dark but radiant, between the body and the soul, thought Gerta. And the image of white clothing hanging out to dry on the balcony came to mind. Karl's soul. Oskar's. And hers.

She believed she had arrived in paradise. An island of warm rocks and cormorants, with waves that launched greenish laps, smacking over the sand. A quiet place, without meetings at the crack of dawn, or the echo of footsteps following you to the foot of your door, or broken glass, or dead animals, or equilateral crosses. An island. A piece of land far from a world on the brink of blowing itself to pieces. Sand and ocean. Pure geography.

They built their tents next to the ruins of Fort Royal's castle, an ancient Gothic fort that was used as a hospital for the wounded during the Crimean War. At night, they'd light a small campfire to cook dinner. And they'd sit with the fire between them.

"A mysterious prisoner lived in those ruins," said Gerta, and a silence that precedes all great tales of the night was created around her. So within that circle of embers, she told the story of the man with the iron mask.

No one was ever completely certain who he was or what he did to be isolated that way. He wore a velvet mask with iron fittings that allowed him to eat with his mask on. Two guards, whose orders were to kill him should he ever try to escape, accompanied him always. Some swore he was the Sun King's twin brother. Others believed he was his bastard brother, son of Anne of Austria and Cardinal Mazarin. The fact was that he was taken to Provence under maximum security. In a locked carriage covered in moleskin. From there, they brought him to this island in a small covered vessel. They say he was taller than most men and with a notable elegance. He dressed in the finest of clothes. They were under strict orders not to deny him anything. And they provided him with the most succulent delicacies. Everything he asked for. And no one could remain seated before him. At night, he would play the guitar with a melancholy that would cause the rocks to shudder. He was buried without his head, so that no one would recognize him even dead.

"He took his secret with him to the grave," concluded Gerta.

André passed her the canteen, looking at her differently, entranced by her voice. In the light of the flames, her face shined as if it were carved in bronze, her head thrown back while she drank, her elbow lifted, pointing to the sky. A drop of water running down her chin. He believed that woman had a gift for telling stories. She was a river. Her words had tact, power of suggestion. He found himself within a halo that surrounded the campfire of twigs.

Is it possible to fall in love with a voice? Up until that moment, André had never found words to be erotic. Never had he thought that talking could be better than fucking, for example. He wasn't very good with words. He felt they had the potential to corner him. With fucking, on the other hand, he was certain this couldn't happen. A good conversationalist can seduce, the words leaving you on the ropes.

"You know a lot of things," he said.

"Alexander Dumas," she said, smiling. "I read *The Vicomte de Bragelonne*, when I was a teenager. It's the third and last book of *The Three Musketeers* saga. Do you like to read?"

"Well, yes, but only books about war . . ."

"Ah . . ." Lifting her eyebrows in a way that suggested slight irony.

She bent over to revive the flame and André could clearly see the triangle of naked skin leading to her cleavage. Smooth, tan, clean-smelling, like saltwater, and he noticed his erection beginning to press up visibly through the fabric of his pants. He wanted to sleep with that woman. He wanted to explore her entire body, open her thighs and enter her, her thoughts, and quiet them with a kiss, and another, and another, until he changed the rhythm of her breathing. Until she could no longer think of anything. He wanted to do all of this once and for all, and stop feeling as he did, cornered by words. That night he learned a metaphor's power of seduction. Somewhere in his head, a strumming of a guitar, so melancholic that even the rocks shuddered, began to break through.

"Good night," she said, lifting herself up and brushing the sand from her pants.

André sat and watched her walk away. Her strong swimmer's back, her flexible movements beneath her cotton shirt, a peculiar sway to her hips when she walked, as if slightly shifting to one side. Arrogance, pride, vanity . . . ancient wisdom of women who know that they're being observed. She brought a branch from the bonfire to her mouth to light a cigarette, took a puff, and he saw her disappear below the canvas covering of the tent.

It was a time for disorder, for physical exaltation, swimming until they collapsed from fatigue on the sand, eating sardines from a can for dinner, going to sleep at the last minute, watching the line on the horizon, the sun burning the night until it disappeared over the ocean's surface. Their heads close together, the smell of the eucalyptus, and the salt on their skin. They fell in love in the South of France—Ruth Cerf would remember later on, trying to reconstruct the fragile thread of their lives for an American journalist—they became inseparable on Île Sainte-Marguerite. A time of one world outside the world, of altered schedules, of days without a date, of gestures followed by shared laughs, complicities between them that didn't allow room for anyone else. Willi Chardack and Raymond Gorin understood immediately. How could they not? Willi and Raymond would go back to their tents quietly at night, while Gerta and André stayed conversing in hushed voices, creating the perfect depth of field around them. There was a secret space between them. A minimum distance, like two pages in a closed book. The scar on his left brow, a blow from a stone. The vaccination mark on her arm, a half-moon precisely where the syringe shot its serum. Marking her skin years ago, in a Stuttgart school gymnasium, when she was eight years old. The list of wounds. His Achilles' heel sticking out of the sleeping bag like an island. A prominent scar on the back of André's hand.

"It's my life line," he joked. "I was born with six fingers. They removed the sixth one shortly after I was born. The midwife assured my mother that it was a sign of good luck. As you can see . . . it's going to turn out she was right."

We always fall in love with a story, not a name or a body but what is inscribed in the man.

In the shade of the eucalyptus trees, Gerta used sand to scrub the bottom of the pot they used to heat the water for the tea. The copper squeaked beneath her fingers. She was barefoot, squatting, wearing an old button-down shirt over her bathing suit. The effects of the sunlight and the great outdoors had turned the ends of her hair a shade or two blonder; there was no longer a trace of the red henna. The sun had dried up a scab on her knee that began to bleed again when she'd bent her leg. She had slipped and hurt herself on the rock moss. With her eyes, she followed the slow trail of blood running toward the instep of her foot. A striking scarlet color that the clotting darkened over the fine hairs of her skin. Without a word, he crouched down at her side, brought his mouth to her knee, and licked the blood. What he would have liked to have said he couldn't say to a woman whose aperture was like an open wound, a youth that was not yet mortal. So he leaned forward and simply lowered his mouth to her wound. Blood. A limited depth of field. His body felt empty. The only thing that felt alive was the consciousness of his desire. How her blood had tasted would be the last thing he'd remember many years later—close to Hanoi, less than a mile away from their fort in Doai Than—during an ambush by the Viet Minh along a road loaded with mines. By then, he was no longer a boy in love but a veteran reporter with more than five wars behind him. And extremely tired of living without her.

"Come," said Gerta, taking him by the hand.

He stood up slowly, without placing his arms around her yet, his mouth very close to hers, barely apart, but without touching, until neither one of them could stand that proximity anymore. Eyes open, fixated on one another, the last rays of sunlight filtering themselves through the leaves of the trees when he brought her to his chest, squeezing her deep, feeling her strong, elastic muscles under her blouse pulse when he covered her face with his hand and placed his salty fingers into her mouth. Arm in arm they walked to the tent, still searching for one another, craving the other with a repressed hunger, a pair of lips thirsty for the saliva and oxygen of the other pair, their teeth colliding from impatience.

"Slow down," she said firmly, separating herself a few inches so she could breathe. Her fingers scratching the sand in André's hair. The ocean and all its mysteries surrounding them.

He dove into her as if into the well of a grotto. Taking his time, aware, firm, without rushing, like she had asked him to. Intuitive, attentive to all of the impulses of the living body below his. Naked, smelling of young sex and the sea. Saliva. Salt. Blood. Bodily fluids that became the only necessities for being alive. From within that vertigo, she floated semiconsciously. Feeling she was about to fall from a high place. Speaking so softly, it was as if she were praying: *Yahweh, Elohim, Adonai, Roi* . . . She grabbed on to his body, pressing him down harder between her muscles, about to fall from high above, breathless. *Whoever you are and wherever you are* . . . She stared into those gorgeous Gypsy eyes and that's when she saw him lift a hand, as if signaling for a truce. Wait, he whispered. Don't move, stay still, please. Don't even breathe. Teeth clenched, in total concentration, trying to regain control of his body. She could feel that he was very deep, wet from her, very hard, and remaining still. Suddenly he plunged again, slowly. This time to the hilt, even farther. Eyeing her closely as he kissed her, resisting pleasure with great difficulty. Prolonging every tremble, aware of her body, tense, moist. With every lunge the pace grew faster. Pressing up against her with more intensity, transporting her to that nonexistent place where every woman wants to be taken. Although she rejects it with her head or complains like a wounded lioness, blessing or cursing or blaspheming with her thoughts and with her eyes and with her voice. *Elohim, Adonai, Roi, Olam, I'm not asking you to save me. I don't need your blessing.* He looked at her, defenseless, the way one would look at a prisoner. He kissed her on the mouth, the marrow of his bones shivering, while she finished praying, faltering, like in dreams, with words that sprouted from some hidden place within, in Yiddish . . . *I only ask that this be real* . . . And in that very moment, she felt him pull out and erupt at the last minute over her stomach.

"Thank you," she said in a low voice, gently caressing his back, without specifying if it was directed at him or the Lord of Hosts, the ruler of foolish chance and of beautiful nights, the implacable legislator of causes and of their ultimate consequences, the God of Abraham and all of the Jews.

Chapter Nine

Maria Eisner was an old acquaintance of André's. She founded Alliance Photo, one of the most prestigious agencies of the time due to its specialization in art and travel but especially because of its photojournalism. She was efficient, a problem-solver, German through and through, with a good managerial sense and gifted nose for detecting who was fit for doing business. It was precisely this that caused her to take notice of Gerta when André introduced them one September afternoon at an outside table at Chez Capoulade. They had just returned from the island and were radiant. Their arms around one another, suntanned, their future awaiting them, and one that would not lack funds. A few of Gerta's remarks on a recent feature in *Europe* magazine were enough for Maria to realize that the girl had vision. It didn't matter if she lacked the technical skills. Those things are learned. What drew Maria was Gerta's point of view. Alliance Photo had emerged with a clear artistic mission. And they were searching for a new perspective. A modern one, along the lines of the architectural vanguard that had been born on the sixth floor of a building on Rue de Sevres, where Le Corbusier established his canon with the frigidness of a Swiss watchmaker. They sought the strange, with a desire to break away from lines and volumes and show reality from a rarely seen perspective. And Gerta had that, along with the advantage of speaking several languages and a sixth sense for business. In less than a month, she learned how to present the material and negotiate the highest price with an aggressive sales technique. The law of supply and demand. She was shrewd when it came to balancing the books, and that proved essential for a company that lived on supplying content to the leading French, Swiss, and North American magazines. It was her big break.

It was as if they had been shipwrecked. She and André, two castaways who had finally found a ship to board and could feel the vibrations of the motor below deck. That thrill of the open-sea journey that awaited them. Their coffee's aroma mixing with the salty breeze, as they bent over to look at a nautical chart freshly spread out over the table. With all the time in the world ahead of them to decide—with enthusiasm, precision, and luck—the exact path, thereafter, to take their lives on.

They moved to a small studio on Rue de Varenne, which barely fit a bathroom, a bed, and a cooking stove. But when they opened their window at night while having dinner, they could see the lights of the Eiffel Tower, and all of Paris's air entered their home with its bridges, tangled-up streets, and autumn plazas.

The afternoon had gone dim, and an aquamarine shade of an American night illuminated the buildings' cornices hanging within the clouds, and the mansard roofs in the distance. An orange glow from the streetlamps lit up their room. A round table, an open newspaper, a sofa covered with a gray cloth, and Gerta's profile, with all of its arrises, beneath the floor lamp. Silent, pensive.

André did not like seeing her like this. It was as if she had escaped to her past world, where he couldn't make her happy. As if, deep down, her Polish-Jewish skepticism was still wary of all that happiness. There was something strange about the way she looked at you, something evasive about it, as if one eye was looking back and the other at the path she was considering taking. He knew there had been other men in her life, of course he did. He had heard talk about Georg hundreds of times when they were just friends. And he had seen a photo of him she stored in a box of quince candy. Blond and much taller than he was, with an aviator's or a polo champion's attitude that wore on André's nerves. He had also had other women. But now he couldn't stand the idea that she'd think back upon her days with the Russian, not even for a second. As if life could cut itself into pieces, as with a knife and a Camembert cheese. Before and now. Of course he freely expressed his jealousy, and often. Perhaps it wasn't entirely jealousy, but complete animal possessiveness. A need to erase the past, an absurd macho pride, a thousand-year-old instinct dating back to when men in hordes howled at the moon at midnight alongside their tribe's campfire. Selecting their female, separating her from the rest to make her exclusively his. So he could bring her to one of those huge prairies of grain and nail a child into her entrails.

"Wouldn't you like to have a baby Gypsy?" he asked softly, trying to take her out of her abstraction. "A screaming, misbehaving child, like me?" He half-smiled, with a touch of slyness at the edge of his lips, but his eyes were serious and loyal, like a cocker spaniel's.

"And as hairy?" she teased, wrinkling up her nose. She shook her head no and laughed loudly, as if she had just heard something completely ludicrous. But afterward, while she looked at the lights of the Eiffel Tower, bright and promising for some, her smile transformed into an expression that was almost sad. It seemed that somewhere in those green eyes with yellow flecks, there lived the feeling that there wasn't a lot of time left for that. As if she truly felt she'd be missing out on the serene pleasure of raising a dark-haired child with Hungarian eyes and pink fingers. Of hanging out his white diapers to dry on a terrace somewhere in the world and telling him a story about a pirate with a parrot on his shoulder, an authentic one from Guiana, that in her version would whistle the "Turkish

March," in honor of Captain Flint. And each night, watch him sleep peacefully with a pacifier, curled up in his crib. A dream.

She looked him straight in the face as if she had just returned from another world. Seeing him there, at her side, so close, looking right back at her with a mixture of tenacity and confusion that profoundly moved her, causing her to believe she was deeply falling in love with this man and had to make an effort to contain herself and not hold him tight and kiss him too many times on his eyes, on his forehead, his neck, behind his ears . . . Because she understood that one day, perhaps before she knew it, that love would make her weak and vulnerable. But back then, there was no way of knowing. She would not have been able to ever imagine that in just a few months she'd remember that conversation, word for word, gesture for gesture, while contemplating from afar not the elegant frame of the Eiffel Tower and its flashing bulbs but Madrid's sky, pierced by the lights of reflectors intersecting, spinning at different angles, while the deafening wails of sirens and the engines of enemy planes roared in the nearby distance. The tight staccato of antiaircraft fire. How on earth was a baby to sleep with all that war racket?

It had barely been a month since Gerta and André had camped on Île Sainte-Marguerite, running barefoot on beaches, discovering the depths of their new love. In Paris, the French Popular Front had consolidated itself with support from the leading parties of the Left, the unions, and all of the groups that formed part of the National Joint Committee of the Popular Front. At the last demonstration commemorating July 14, thousands of workers, standing beneath portraits of Marx and Robespierre, gathered to shout out the lyrics to the *"Marseillaise"* at the top of their lungs. Radio Paris retransmitted the reconciliation between the Republic's tricolored flag and the red flag of hope, for the entire world to listen. A unified action against Fascism had become the number-one priority.

Among intellectuals, l'Association des Écrivains et Artistes Révolutionnaires served as one of the front's principal supporters since its unification. Some of the surrealists, who had grown tired of chasing their interior ghosts, had touched ground again in order to face the pressing reality of a world on the verge of collapse. Even the most idealistic of the poets began to seriously ask themselves if the time hadn't come to join the Communist Party. Gerta wasn't a Communist, but she was well versed in their politics. After all, she had learned it firsthand from an authentic Russian Bolshevik. Georg was the first to teach her the mysteries of Marxism-Leninism when she was still an adolescent who dreamt of being Greta Garbo. André, on the other hand, leaned toward Trotskyism or the ideas of the anarchists, which were far better suited to his independent nature, his propensity for walking on edges, his addiction to the dangers of raw nights.

More than ever, the old cafés had become forums for heated debate. Everyone was ready to lend a hand. Painters, writers, refugees, photographers . . . The naughty-eyed Pablo Picasso, ready to charge like a bull, and the always provocative Dora Maar on her eternal honeymoon; Man Ray, short, enigmatic, addicted to his work as well as to Lee Miller, the most beautiful American in Paris, ultra-tall, blond, and fickle, the woman who cleaved his soul in two; Henri Matisse and his very serious wife with a face as long as a horse's; Luis Buñuel, born in Aragón, with that rock-hard head of his, listening to jazz at the Mac-Mahon, then meeting Jeanne Rucar, whom he would marry after forcing her to throw the little gold cross she wore around her neck into the Seine; Ernest Hemingway and Martha Gellhorn, always on the brink of destruction, competitive, capable of battling against each other or both of them against the world, with their own style of guerrilla warfare. Complicated couples. A far cry from traditional marriages, where wide-hipped women were kept like caged prisoners in their wire corsets, patiently ironing their husbands' shirts. Just left of the Seine River, a new concept of love had been born: conflicted, dangerous, like walking barefoot in a jungle. Gerta and André felt right at home in that scene. It was as if they were part of one big eccentric family.

The Left's joint program, in turn, expressed itself with a few basic points: amnesty for the prisoners, the right to freely form unions, a reduction in the work week, the dissolution of paramilitary organizations, and promotion of peace within the League of Nations. But on October 3—a day like any other and without any prior war declarations—100,000 soldiers from the Italian army, led by General De Bono, attacked Emperor Haile Selassie's Ethiopian troops. Tanks and mustard gas against bows and arrows. The League of Nations imposed small sanctions on Italy, but Great Britain and France continued selling them oil, even after they learned Italians had attacked Red Cross hospitals and ambulances.

"Europe is asleep." André banged his fist on the table. His brow gathered, his voice firm, speaking from the platform at Chez Capoulade. Gerta had never seen him give a political speech before, but she decided she preferred him like this: furious, his eyes bright with indignation, fiery, charismatic, almost violent, with a large vein throbbing in his neck as he denounced Mussolini's methods of lowering the morale of the people of Ethiopia. "They are violating the Geneva Convention."

However, as strange as it may seem, the news of the world didn't completely spoil that enchanting autumn of 1935, with its streets covered in yellow leaves and women as thin as reeds smoking in jazz clubs until dawn. It was filled with movie theaters and bookstores and storefronts, where on one afternoon, Gerta discovered *Le Temps du Mépris* by André Malraux, a writer who was also devoted body and soul to the anti-Fascist movement. On some nights, when André was asleep, or after she had read awhile, she would get up, throw one of his shirts over her shoulders, and sneak over to the window to smoke her last cigarette. Paris and its lights in the distance. That October climate of longing made it hard for her to sleep. It also happened to her when she was a child. Just as she was getting ready for bed was when she'd feel most alive. She'd recount the day's events in her head and, using a pencil, write them down in a school notebook in her child's handwriting, using the eraser when she made a mistake. She needed that structure. The day did not feel finished until she reached that moment. It was as if she put her thoughts to rest when she wrote. Trying to understand them. Needing to return to them in order to orient herself. It was a moment just for her, where no one else could enter, not friends, not lovers.

"There are those whom we cannot even embrace," she wrote. "Or at least scratch or bite to keep your sanity in their company. There are times I'd like to grab André by the hair as if he were drowning and have him cling to me. Sometimes the dream is different. It's a nightmare that happens in the moonlight. In the dream I'm walking toward him, along an unfamiliar street, and just as I'm about to reach him, smiling, my hand raised to greet him, something happens. I'm not sure what, something urgent and inexplicable that forces me to run as fast as I can, to even climb over the wall at the dead end, and disappear. I don't know what it could mean. The street, the wall, a moonlight so white, like a cold star . . . Perhaps I should ask René. There is something about love that short-circuits. As if we have to read the same paragraph twice in order to find a connection between the sentences. It's a wild feeling that bursts into the other's routine like a gale wind, causing everything to fly all over the place, like a house being aired out in the midst of a storm. It wants to erase everything. Re-create it, as if the world didn't exist before it."

She shut the notebook and placed it in the drawer of her nightstand. She needed to rid herself of her thoughts.

Chapter Ten

R eady, one, two, three. Gerta and Ruth each grabbed an end of the board and placed it onto the two easels. A string of colorful lanterns hung from the ceiling of their Rue Lobineau flat. They were getting ready for a surprise party for André's birthday. October 22. The same day as John Reed's.

Ten Days That Shook the World left a strong impression on Gerta. She could still remember the book's red cover on top of the table at the lake house, next to a vase of tulips, the white tablecloth, and everything else.

She considered it a first-class testimony and could recite entire paragraphs by heart. That was the kind of journalism she and André yearned to do. To be right in the center of the events, seeing them firsthand, feeling the heart of the world pump through its veins.

They covered the entire length of the table with white sheets. Ruth cooked a traditional *lekaj* in the oven. Honey, raisins, almonds, and cloves, just like it's served on the Jewish New Year. She spent hours preparing it. Henri brought two bottles of Calvados from his native Normandy.

Twenty-two. The two little ducks. An unforgettable birthday. All kinds of drinks, laughter until dawn, champagne, candles, cigarettes, paper lanterns, photographs out of focus. Henri Cartier-Bresson and Chim covered in streamers, drinking straight out of the bottle of Calvados. Hiroshi Kawazoe and Seiichi Inoue, two Japanese artists they had met on Île Sainte-Marguerite, who performed a traditional samurai dance. Willi Chardack dressed up as the man with the iron mask. Fred Stein, completely drunk, clowning around, his arms around a broomstick. Csiki Weiss and Geza Korvin, with their fists in the air. Comrades of André's, two old friends from his years in Budapest, of the heroic times of stealing croissants from the bars of shops recently opened in Paris. Chim, frowning again, concentrated, trying to build an Eiffel Tower with toothpicks. The journalist Lotte Rapaport swearing never again to accept another job as a seamstress. Paris was full of lunatics. Gerta, cut out against the light of the window, wearing a tight pair of pants and a black turtleneck, laughing with her head thrown back. André's profile in the gangster hat he'd been given. That cigarette appended to the corner of his mouth. The laughter in his eyes, that air of mischief. "Happy Birthday," she said into his ear, softly. Their faces close, dancing to a new cabaret tune that was becoming fashionable on the radio. It was sung by a young girl who was as slight as a sparrow, named Edith Piaf. They were bidding farewell to their childhood. And they did not know it.

That's how they passed the time. On other occasions, they'd stroll through the *quais* of the Seine. Gerta loved looking at the boats all lit up along the waterfront. A boat is always a promising possibility. When they received an assignment's paycheck, they'd treat themselves to coffee and croissants at the cafés near Place Renée Vivien. Sometimes she'd accompany André on one of his photo shoots. That's how she began her training. Setting the focus, calculating the exposure time, adjusting the diaphragm to the light. She liked to watch André lean up against the wall and mentally prepare the photo he planned to take. And though she had randomly arrived at photography, she grew increasingly fascinated with everything about it. The smell of the developing fluid. The tension of waiting and watching your own face appear, bit by bit, at the bottom of the tray. Those small and bony fingers holding her chin, the arch of a raised clavicle over the delicate skin on her neckline. The darkest shadows below her eyes. The mystery.

Sometime later, Georg sent her a postcard from Italy. A scene from Florence's Piazza della Signoria, taken from the Loggia dei Lanzi. André didn't want to read it but spent the entire day squinting his eyes like a bull in heat, responding to her questions with monosyllables. If she offered him a cigarette, he preferred not to smoke; if she pointed out a red carnation in one of the stalls along the Left Bank, he looked the other way. Just another damn ordinary flower.

Gerta could sense the storm coming and tried to tiptoe around the thunder to avoid it. It would pass. Thankfully, she had enough work to do so as not to agonize over it so much.

She had been able to negotiate several contracts for Alliance Photo at a good price. Maria Eisner was thrilled with her. She worked hard, having slept less than five hours a night over the last few weeks. Yes, she would have preferred if the 1,200 francs she was being paid a month were for her photographs and not for her bookkeeping. But it was all there was, and she couldn't complain. Besides, she never backed away from an opportunity to push André's work. She fought for each and every one of his photographs as if her life depended on it. That same morning, she had negotiated a 1,100 franc advance for three assignments per week for him. It wasn't a lot, given the high price of the materials he needed, but it was enough for him to pay his rent, eat a decent meal three times a day, or treat himself to something extra once in a while. That's what passed through her mind as she walked the frozen streets back home with her hands shoved deep into her coat pockets, sporting a wool hat and a red nose from the cold, like an Arctic explorer. I may not be perfect, she thought with a hint of condescension aimed at herself, but as a manager I'm not bad at all. Deep down, she was proud and wanted to get home and deliver the news to André. She wanted to feel his arms around her waist, his body pressed up against hers, transmitting heat, taking her to high and faraway places, slowly, waiting for her as no one else ever had.

It was late. She found him facedown on the bed, hair disheveled, one side of his face against the pillow, and fresh stubble darkening his jawline. In order not to wake him, she quietly removed her clothes and placed them on a hook behind the door. Then she put on an old gray undershirt that she always wore to bed and, looking for the warmth of his body, curled up against André's back.

It was like hugging a jackal. He let out a terrible growl. The animal inside him had been awakened and it almost caused her to fly off the bed and onto the floor.

"Can you tell me what in hell is the matter with you?" she asked.

Nothing. A deathly silence, nocturnal, withdrawn in thought. Mute as God's shadow. Gerta flipped herself over to face the wall. She didn't feel like fighting.

"You Hungarians are strange," she said.

"True," he said, "but never as idiotic as the Russians."

At last the jackal had come out of his cave. A feeling of terrible disgust and immense exhaustion came over her, and she thought to herself that neither of them deserved what was about to happen. Because she suddenly knew that when he lifted his head, he'd look at her exactly the way he was looking at her now: his face severe, distant, his naked arm spread across the sheet. She wasn't certain by way of her mind but through her body and the goose bumps on her skin that foretold what he would say, word for word, in a harsh tone, his voice unrecognizable. And while she listened to his string of stupidities, the kind men have repeated hundreds of times to women—in every kind of room, in every part of the world—that's when she felt the boiling blood flowing within her face. It's him or me. It's here or there. It's black or white. She thought he'd be different, but no. As absurd as any of them. Ridiculously simple. Capable of throwing it all away for nothing, for stupid male pride that can't appreciate what it has and wants more. To be the only one. Only him. Nobody else, not now, not before, not never. Sure, then go ahead, walk out that door and go back in time ten years. When I was still a sweet girl, and there still was no trace of a vase with white tulips, or a small house on the lake, or a damn pistol on top of the table, or salesclerks who throw anyone out of their stores by pushing them, or going out at the crack of dawn to distribute pamphlets through the streets of Leipzig, or Georg, or Wächterstrasse, or anything, not one thing, nothing. I mean who did that Gypsy think he was? Did the world begin when he was born? For the love of God.

She stormed out of their bed, unable to believe what she was hearing. Because now he didn't have her cornered, nor was he forcing her to make odious and uncouth comparisons. Who's better? Who was worse? How did he do it to you? Like I do it? What he wanted was to hurt, offend, and humiliate. That's why he brought out that photograph that appeared in *Vogue* of Regina Langquarz, tall, with short hair and legs like a heron. In fact, had she ever asked him about her? Didn't matter. There he was, telling it all in great detail, offering explanations that no one had asked for. Or about the Spaniard he met while he was in Tossa del Mar while he was on assignment with *Berliner Illustrierte*. You damn Hungarian bastard. Damn the very sight of you. I never want to see you again in my life. Stupid vain bastard. Bastard. Bastard. Bastard . . . This was what was running through Gerta's mind as she rushed to put her pants and her shirt back on. Her lips trembling, she was overcome with a nausea that forced her to lean up against the wall and place her hands over her mouth.

He looked at her from the bed as someone would at a film that was being projected. But one where the reel, at some moment, had come undone, and it was now impossible to rewind or to find a way back that wasn't rigged with mines of pride. He would have given anything to be able to stop her, to grab her by the arm and look her straight in the eye, without resorting to the words that always cornered him but, rather, to their bodies. That was the language he felt safe in. He wanted to kiss her mouth and her nose and her eyelids and afterward push her onto the bed and enter her, firm and steady, dominating her at his own rhythm, until reaching that place that was exclusively his, where there wasn't room for other men or other women, the past or the future, where you couldn't find Georg Kuritzkes or Regina Langquarz to stand in the way. But he was left paralyzed, scratching his chin, wrinkling his forehead, with his head against the wall and a weightlessness in his stomach. He had a strong sensation that every second that passed was being played out against him. That he should say or do something soon. Anything. Regardless, he still waited until the last moment for her to be the one to do it. In some things women are infinitely stronger than men. He realized he had ruined everything when it was already too late; when he saw her grab her coat from the rack and slam the door before bolting down the stairs, two at a time.

Snow. All of Paris was covered in snow. The rooftops, the streets, the fences, the barges protected by pneumatic wheels that traversed the Seine, beneath a sky so gray that from a distance it could be mistaken for the cloudy surface of the river, the color of lead, with dark green veins, and as desolate as the Danube on a winter evening. He searched everywhere for days. Ruth's house, Chim's. Going up and down the café route a million times without any luck. La Coupole, Le Cyrano, Les Deux Magots, Le Palmier, the Café de Flore . . . nothing. The earth had swallowed her whole. André walked the snowy streets like a phantom. Overcoat buttoned to the top, his collar up, listening to the ubiquitous murmur of Christmas carols and the small bells that children shook in doorways asking for pastries and sweets. With an infinite melancholy, his eyes gravitated toward steamed-up windows with lace curtains, behind which he imagined warm and cozy homes. He was discovering the oldest reasons why people choose to uproot themselves. Remembering how the streets of Pest looked to him when he was six or seven years old and he lived on 10 Városház Utca, in the back part of a block with apartments that had hallways and staircases with banisters. Back then, he liked dreaming with his eyes open and his nose glued to the toy shop windows located in stately neighborhoods where the grand palaces of the Austro-Hungarian Empire still stood strong on the other side of the river. Although he sensed Saint Nicholas wasn't going to leave any of those magnificent locomotives beside his stocking under the chimney. Because Christian saints didn't have any jurisdiction in the Jewish district. And besides, the postal service didn't deliver mail to working-class neighborhoods. There were certain things worth knowing as soon as possible. Who you are. Where you come from. Where you're headed. That's why, at fifteen, he chose to side with the world's disinherited. Of course he thought about her. All the time. Morning and night. Picturing her dressed and undressed. With shoes or barefoot. Lying on the sofa wearing a shirt that just reached her thighs, and a bunch of photographs on her lap, without any makeup on, with that sexy, indolent air she had just waking up that drove him wild. This is what he thought about as he walked under the star of Bethlehem that hung over the Boulevard des Capucines, and saw himself reflected in the storefront windows of pastry shops full of adorned marzipans with tricolored cockades and candied chestnuts. He saw shops decked in mistletoe, the stalls covered in poinsettias, and he wanted to die. His shoulders hunched, his hands shoved down deep in his pockets. Wearing two layers of socks and a coat lined with lamb fur didn't make a difference: he was dying from the cold. To him it seemed worse than the glacial winters in Hungary. He walked on. An iciness in his soul. Mad at himself, adrift, his gait erratic, moving clumsily and getting pushed by the crowds of people carrying packages and walking in the opposite direction. He felt a blind rage against the world. A few times, he shoved back without excusing himself and when he had to face one indignant passerby, he limited himself to kicking the edge of the sidewalk.

"Fucking Christmas."

Chapter Eleven

It wasn't clear how he died, but all indications pointed to suicide. Gerta found out from Ruth. She knew André adored his father. Deep down, he and his father were one and the same. Dreamy, imaginative, capable of believing their own lies to the point of converting them into truths. In fact, many of the tales that André liked to entertain his friends with were simply new versions of the stories that, as a child, he had heard his father tell at the Café Moderno in Pest, when he was sent by his mother to go and bring him home before he spent all of the family's savings in one game of pinnacle.

Dezső Friedmann, like André, was an incurable romantic, who had grown up in the depths of rural Transylvania sheltered by folk tales and medieval legends. When he was barely an adolescent, without a duro to his name, he abandoned that place to see the world, surviving in his travels from city to city thanks to his picaresque ingenuity. Until one day he met Júlia, André's mother, and he decided to become a tailor.

André would listen to his worldly adventures with eyes as wide as saucers, feeling proud and amused, like when Dezső told him that he used a Budapest restaurant bill as his visa to cross the border. He tried to imagine him there, looking very serious, taking out the documents from the inside pocket of his jacket with an air of authority, and this would throw André into a fit of laughter. Many years later, André himself would use the same ruse to leave Berlin and it had also worked for him. One's luck is also inherited.

His father would always say that to be a good gambler, you had to always act as if you had an ace up your sleeve. If you play the part of the winner well, you end up winning the game. The bad part is that sometimes life calls your bluff ahead of schedule. Leaving no choice but to bet what's left on your last hand. Dezső lost it all.

Like hair color or belief in omens, gambling is a secret illness that's carried in one's genes. André had that gene in his veins. When things weren't going well for him, he'd spend his time drinking and placing bets. Henri Cartier-Bresson, with his infallible Norman eye, would often say: André was never the most intelligent of men. His talent was never pondering the intellectual root of a concept, but he was an incredibly intuitive player. He had an eye for details that the rest of us could not see. I suppose that experience also helped sharpen his sense of smell. Since the age of seventeen, he'd been on his own, moving from one hotel to the next, and later from one war to the next. He was born a gambler.

The man did not lack reason, as he would show many years later, on the morning of June 6, 1944, while the fog tore to shreds the sky over the English Channel.

Ocean. The sound of the ocean. It was impossible to focus with all that movement. Above, the rattle of the machines, the fear on deck. Below, the foaming abyss of the waves. André didn't think twice. He jumped into the landing craft with his two Contax cameras around his neck. Then he looked toward the beach and tried to calculate the depth and distance that they were planning. Up ahead, three miles of sand planted with mines. Omaha Beach. Nobody had explained to those boys what the hell they were supposed to do there. Only that they should save Europe from the clutches of the Nazis. As they approached the shore, he winked at a young American soldier from Company E of 116th Infantry Regiment. "See you there, kid," he said, trying to lift his spirits.

Minutes later, the world blew to pieces. The majority of the boys hadn't reached their twenties yet. Shot down before setting one foot on the sand. In the focus, flashes of orange amid thousands of particles of water spray. An anti-tank trap. A mortar blast. A roaring sea. Orders given that were almost drowned out by the wind and the motorboats. He just kept shooting; there was no time to stop and adjust the focus. Snapshots, fast and fleeting. *Images of War.* Afterward, the Atlantic's whipped foam was dyed red in the worst bloodbath of D-Day. Two thousand dead in under two hours.

André was the only photographer to disembark during the first wave. Voluntarily, he enlisted with the 116th. In Easy Red. "The war correspondent has his stake—his life—in his own hands," he wrote in his book *Slightly Out of Focus.* "And he can put it on this horse or that horse, or he can put it back in his pocket at the very last minute. I am a gambler. I decided to go in with Company E in the first wave." It's a miracle he survived while trying to advance in water up to his neck and, later, while dragging himself through 125 miles of sand that had mines. A game of cat and mouse. Of course, by then his name was no longer André Friedmann and she was no longer at his side. She'd been dead for seven years. Seven long years in which there was never a single day or a damn night that he didn't long for her. Perhaps the only thing he wanted was for someone to take pity on him and shoot him already.

Gerta was also familiar with this way of thinking. It's either this or that. Here or there. Dead or alive. When it comes down to it, life is a game of chance. She walked by the bars across from the Petit Pont and saw his back through the window. She knew she'd find him there. He was alone, standing there, motionless, wearing a coat that looked like it was made for someone a lot more corpulent, his arm crossed on top of the counter, his head lowered, lost in thought. Breaking his stillness only to lift a glass to his lips. It was still before eleven in the morning. As sad as a tree from which they had just shot down a robin, she thought to herself, feeling the tears begin to cloud her vision. She cursed herself, as she always did when this happened, though she wasn't sure for whom she was crying. She was about to start running in the direction she'd come from. But a force greater than her will kept her there, and so she waited for the air to dry her eyes. Then took a deep breath, resorted to all the haughtiness that her father had taught her, and went to find her man with her head held high and in her peculiar manner of walking. Relieved to have found him, but also determined not to yield an inch of her territory before him.

"It's so cold," she said, hunching her shoulders, just standing there next to him with her clenched fists in her pockets.

He raised his eyebrows.

"Where were you?" he asked in a tone somewhat guarded.

"Around," she said. And she remained silent.

That's how it happened. Without one overly surprising the other, without big declarations or an unnecessary show of emotion. In a certain way, it was natural, as if they had simply resumed a dialogue that had been temporarily interrupted. Each had traveled their stretch of the road.

"It'd be better if we headed back home, right?" she said again after some time had passed. And they slowly began walking along the sidewalk. He, glued to the walls, trying to walk a straight line. She, discreetly guiding him, so as not to humiliate him.

They began living together again. Moving out of the Eiffel Tower apartment and into the Hôtel de Blois on Rue Vavin. They could see Le Dôme Café from their window. All they had to do was poke their head out to see who had gathered and go downstairs if the clientele was to their liking. Although the truth was that between the electoral campaign and the reports for Alliance Photo, they no longer had too much time to sit around talking.

In February, the French authorities conceded special work permits that would assure journalists residency. Gerta believed it was the only way to legalize her status. She obtained her very first press accreditation signed by the head of the ABC Press Service of Amsterdam. In her identity card photo, she appears happy, wearing a leather jacket, her chin slightly raised, her hair blond, short, and falling over her forehead on one side. A proud smile. February 4, 1936. To Gerta, that document was far more than a legal safeguard. It was her passport as a journalist.

Though she began publishing her first chronicles and selling a few photographs, she never stopped thinking as the manager she had promised to be. They needed the money. And selling pieces solely on political matters wouldn't have allowed them to pay the rent. So they combined it with other kinds of assignments, small ones, about Parisian life in the budding springtime, when everything was waiting to happen. Street markets and places located on the outskirts of the city were where André most liked to go. It was where he felt the most comfortable. Marginal venues like the Crochet Theater, an open-air performance place run by two unscrupulous talent scouts. People would act out scenes in front of a camera and a live audience. There were Fred Astaire and Ginger Rogers impersonators who'd sweat their guts out when they danced. Ambitious young people who wanted to conquer the world, and cabaret entertainers on military reserve, broken by life and looking for a way out. André sympathized with them. At the end of every performance, the implacable audience would show their approval or rejection by their applause or booing. As always, he limited himself to photographing emotions. He knew what he was looking for and he always found it. In Paris or Madrid. In Normandy or Vietnam. During Bastille Day celebrations or on the outskirts of the Crochet Theater. His objective was directed at the interior of each face. His camera captured the emotion and held it within. It didn't matter if it was a tired old man walking off the stage with his head hung low in times of peace or a militia woman with a ladle in her hand serving soup from a pot in the midst of war. It was the same style. To go where no one else was able to go: a couple greeting each other euphorically from the stage; two children sitting on the pavement playing marbles, a house behind them destroyed by the bombings. A dark-eyed ballerina's Gypsy dance of fire through the air; two elderly British men drinking tea at a shelter on Waterloo Road during a German attack in 1941. The head and the tail of a coin. Emotions.

It was months of hard work. The days were long and draining, and they arrived at their hotel exhausted. On a few occasions, they fell right to sleep still fully dressed. Lying diagonally over their bed, embracing, one side of her face on his stomach, like two children who had just arrived home from a long trip. Somewhere a war was approaching like a raven wing that would enter through the attic window.

There were too many debts to pay off, photographic materials were expensive, and newspapers took forever to pay. There was also Cornell. After André's father died, his younger brother, Cornell, came to live with them in Paris. He was a shy and skinny sixteen-year-old with bony shoulders and a squirrel face. He had arrived with the idea of studying medicine but ended up like all of them, developing photos in the bathroom bidet. Somehow they had to find a new way of making money. Gerta couldn't stop thinking about it. And then, it suddenly came to her. It was exactly what they needed. A stroke of genius.

They invented a character, a man named Robert Capa, a supposed American photographer, who was rich, famous, and talented. The dreamer in André loved the name. Sonorous. Short. Easy to pronounce in any language. As well as reminding him of the movie director, Frank Capra, who had made a sweep at the Oscars with *It Happened One Night*, starring Claudette Colbert and Clark Gable. It was a cinematic pseudonym, cosmopolitan, difficult to determine a specific territory, hard to classify within any ethnic or religious group. The perfect name for a nomad without a country.

She also changed her identity. My name is Taro. Gerda Taro. The same vowels as her favorite actress, Greta Garbo. The same syllables. The same music. While it could equally be a Spanish name, Swedish, or Balkan. And it was anything but Jewish.

"What kind of world do we live in if you can't even choose your own name," she'd say.

Once more, it was all a game. An innocent imposture that came from the heart. Divide yourself in two, become someone else, act. Just like she did as a little girl in her house in Stuttgart when she imitated silent film actresses in her attic.

The actors were clear. All they needed was a good argument for making the movie, and they found it. André would take the photos, Gerda would sell them, and this so-called Robert Capa would bring with him the fame. But because he was supposed to be this highly sought-after professional, Gerda would not sell his negatives for less than 150 francs. Three times the going rate. What her mother had taught her proved to be prophetic once again. As was Dezső Friedmann's advice. An air of success begets success.

Sometimes problems would arise, naturally, tiny adjustments to the script, which they managed to cleverly solve. If André wasn't able to get a good shot at the Popular Front rally or the latest Renault strike, Gerda had him covered.

"That Capa bastard took off again with some actress to the Côte d'Azur. Damn him."

But no game is completely harmless. Or innocent. André fully threw himself into the role of Capa. And he wore Capa like a glove. Working hard to be the bold, triumphant American photographer that she wanted him to be. Although somewhere deep down in his soul there was always a trace of melancholy. He wondered which of the two she was truly in love with. André loved Gerta. Gerda loved Capa. And in the end, Capas, like all idols, only love themselves.

His camera was always at all the events, up in the attic at Galeries Lafayette, at the Renault factories, in the stands of the Buffalo arena, or on the sidewalks with more than 100,000 French citizens celebrating the metal workers' victory in the strike. Whether hidden within the masses, at a political meeting, or in the middle of the street, he searched for new perspectives that would allow him to better understand that time of his life that was slipping through his fingers.

Days that moved at a speed of a swallow in flight. They were gulping down the present without realizing it. Feeling so much a part of the world they were living in that they began to let their guard down. Nonetheless, there were people who followed their movements step by step: their first coffee of the day at Le Dôme Café; her hand underneath his shirt on a bus from Saint-Denis; love in a hurry during a taxi ride from the Pont Neuf to the Mac-Mahon club; the sun filtering through Gerta's fingers in the stairwell of Hôtel de Blois, when she covered his face with her hands as he undressed as quickly as he could, a shining look of delirium in his eyes, panting, his mouth searching for hers with urgency, impatience, her fingers struggling tenaciously to unbutton his shirt, his tongue licking the tip of her arrogant chin, as they climbed the stairs toward their third-floor room embracing, pressing up against each other on every landing, out of breath, when finally they were able to stick the key in the lock. An entire network of spies was hovering over them, but love can't see a thing. It's blind. Only Chim, with his experienced Talmudic insight, noticed strange coincidences now and again, an excessive repetition of faces in the same places, discreet convolutions that most likely would not bode well for them.

They, on the other hand, felt confident with their brand-new press credentials and his fabulous persona. They were young, good-looking, unbeatable. As if everything that came before could be erased in one fell swoop. Robert Capa and Gerda Taro at the "Kilometer Zero" of their lives. Could it be possible to imagine a greater dream than this?

Just as had happened in Spain shortly before, on May 3 the Leftist coalition that formed part of the Popular Front arrived at the Élysée Palace, and Robert Capa was there to photograph every second of the euphoria. It had barely been three months since German troops had effortlessly occupied the Rhineland, going against the Treaty of Versailles. All of France shuddered. The Parisians began to mobilize. Thousands of anonymous citizens took to the streets, and their facial expressions were captured in every single one of his photographs: worried, tense, hopeful as they crammed into the Place de l'Opéra to see the electoral results projected on a big screen. Finally, there was a force strong enough to detain the Fascists' advancements. Two-thirds of the house seats were held by Socialists and their top candidate, León Blum, their hero who had survived an attempt on his life by the Fascists in February. Red flags flying over the ministries. Through all of Montparnasse's squares, accordions playing "*L'Internationale.*"

By July, Maria Eisner asked Gerda to negotiate a contract with Capa for a report on the twentieth anniversary of the Battle of Verdun, the bloodiest battle of the First World War. The photographs revealed a bleak scenario: vast areas of no-man's-land covered with charred trees and craters filled with stagnant water. The ceremony was especially emotional. Hundreds of reflectors lit up the military cemetery. Every veteran stood behind a white cross and left a bouquet of flowers over each tomb. In the midst of that silence, a cannon sounded, then the spotlights were turned off and the crowd was left in darkness. There weren't any speeches, either. Just the voice of a four-year-old boy asking for world peace. His appeal, which sounded over loudspeakers placed in all four corners of the cemetery, gave goose bumps to all who were gathered there that evening.

It was of no use. Shortly after their return from Verdun, Gerta and André—that is, Gerda and Capa—had plans to meet some friends for dinner to celebrate the salary increase that had been approved by the Popular Front. They were on the balcony at the Grand Monde, where the bartenders prepared the best cocktails in all the Rive Gauche. She was wearing a backless black dress that gave her a certain air of a Hollywood muse; he a beige jacket and tie. A light breeze rustled the trees along the Seine. July 17. Music, laughter, the clinking of glasses, and then suddenly, once again, in the midst of all that happiness, a raven wing.

From the restaurant's kitchen, through the tiny speaker of a radio device, the news made its way through: an uprising of the Spanish Legion in Morocco under the command of a man named Francisco Franco, a grim, second-rate general. The Spanish imitation of a Hitler or Mussolini.

The countdown had begun.

Chapter Twelve

- two pairs of pants
- three shirts
- underwear
- socks
- a towel
- a comb
- a bar of soap
- razor blades
- sanitary napkins
- the red notebook
- a map
- surgical tape
- aspirin

She was forgetting something, but she didn't know what. Gerda stood in front of her travel bag on top of the bed, placed a finger on her temple to think, and in an instant, she snapped her fingers. Of course. A bilingual Spanish dictionary.

Spain had become the eye of the world's great storm. It was the only topic of conversation. Even the surrealists, who were the least interested in politics, embraced the Republican cause. Gathering groups of friends at various homes around town at the last minute, so they could parse the news that was growing more contradictory and alarming by the hour. Military revolts in the Balearic and Canary Islands. Resistance in Asturias. Someone called Queipo de Llano and an uprising in Sevilla, killings and summary executions in Navarra and Valladolid. The imagery that each saw in their heads reminded them immensely of Goya's Black Paintings. Fiery red and hellish bitumen. That's why, when the systematic bombings began in Madrid, each shell that thundered would also shake the very foundation of Paris. A warning of the cataclysms that were still to come. The streets were buzzing. They all headed to La Coupole and Café de Flore, desiring to know more than what they were reading in the newspapers . . . Some breaking news, a reliable account, anything . . . While the governments of Europe had abandoned the young Spanish Republic, a giant army of men and women had appeared to defend it on their own will and initiative.

There were writers, metal workers, dockers from the Rhine and the Thames, artists, students, the majority of them without military experience but with a deep conviction that the world's greatest battle was brewing on the other side of the Pyrenees. There were also journalists and photographers, dozens of international special correspondents. Loads of refugees who had shared a table and cigarettes with Gerda and Capa many nights at Chez Capoulade and had joined the International Brigade . . . The poet Paul Éluard wrote in *L'Humanité*:

> *One gets used to everything*
> *except these birds of lead*
> *except his hatred for all that shines*
> *except letting them take over.*

Gerda looked out the tiny window. She had never flown on an airplane before. Under the fuselage, the Pyrenees had a faded mauve color to them, like a washed-out shirt, and every hillside appeared to be digging a furrow of shadows as the sun began to set. Lucien Vogel, the editor of *Vu* magazine, had chartered the flight to Barcelona for a small expedition of journalists contributing to a special Civil War issue he was planning to publish. Pure sky, smooth as an aquarium, crystal-clear light with lime-green-colored parhelia. Gerda was absorbed in that space that would soon be covered in stars. "So magnificent," she thought out loud. Capa observed her as if they'd just met. She never appeared more beautiful to him than she did at the moment, her neck resting on the leather of her seat, her bony chin, her dreamy eyes savoring an inexplicable hope.

Sometimes this happened with her, and it caused him to feel left out. He thought he had her, and then suddenly one word or a simple phrase made him realize that in reality, he didn't know what was going through her head at certain times. But he had learned to live with this. It was true that she was faraway, withdrawn. She had returned to Reutlingen when she was five years old, and she was walking back home with her brothers from Jakob's bakery with a poppy-seed cake and condensed milk in their hands for dinner. Three children in wool sweaters, interlinking arms over shoulders, looking up at the sky, while the stars fell, two by two, three by three . . . She had never been as close to them as she'd been back then. That proximity caused her to feel a sense of solitude and sadness. As if somewhere in the world a secret melody sounded that only she could hear. The message of the stars.

You could already see the city lights below, the triangle of Montjuïc getting larger by the minute, the inclined extension of houses, and then the engine delay, when she suddenly felt herself rising up on one side, as if someone had grabbed and pulled her shoulder up. The noise from the engine grew dense, and the five tons of metal began to rock. In the cockpit, the needles of the position indicators began oscillating faster. The fuel pressure decreased. The entire plane shook with furious tremors. Everyone looked at each other without saying a word. We're going to crash, she thought, but there wasn't enough time to feel fear or to ask her god to save them. They were level with the hills now, their eardrums aching due to the pressure change, their heart beating a hundred miles a minute, but silent. They were still alive. The tiny gardens that surrounded the Prat Airport began to shake outside their windows, first on one side, then on the other. The pilot, up in the cockpit, with his head lowered, could no longer distinguish between that big mass of sky and the earth. The man was fully concentrated on trying to control the airplane. He couldn't even see the gyroscope. He tried to avoid the hilltops as best he could, but they were right on top of the plane, and he came to the decision to try and land the plane anywhere he could, even if it risked slamming onto the ground. At five hundred horsepower revolutions per minute, the plane ran through the light path of its own head beams, directly toward the earth. *Adonai, Elohim, Yahweh . . .* Gerda didn't have time for more. Then the red lights of the runway beacon came on and she saw how the plane was trying to lift its nose, and then a wing tilted to one side, slamming against the wall of a shed. The roar was so intense that her ears began to bleed. She saw André gesticulating like a silent film actor. Moving his mouth, screaming something, but she couldn't hear what he was saying. There was a lot of smoke inside the cabin, and the exhaustion had stiffened her muscles. Soon after, firemen, militia, and a truck with a red cross painted on its canvas arrived . . . Vague sounds of voices in a language she didn't understand, confusing murmurs, arms that lifted the wounded. The pilot was taken out on a stretcher. Two reporters were also evacuated with various kinds of fractures; Lucien Vogel himself broke his right arm in three places. But Capa and Gerda were able to exit the craft on their own two feet. A bit stunned and disoriented but unharmed. It would have been better to cross the border through Irún on foot, as Chim had done.

When you leave a bad port behind and you finally touch the ground, it's good to curse, spit out a blasphemy with gusto, send the God of Sinai to hell with his damn Tablets of the Law and his fucking proverbial bullshit. Fuck. Fuck. Fuck . . . was the first thing André did. One feels a lot better afterward.

"Were you frightened?" he asked, passing her a sip of whiskey directly from the bottle that had been offered to them. They were headed to Barcelona in a car that was being driven by a militiaman in a blue uniform with military suspenders crossed over his chest and two cartridges on his belt.

"No," she said, without intending to boast. And she wasn't trying to appear brave; it's just she didn't have time. Fear needs a rested conscience. It wasn't a foreign feeling to her. She knew all its symptoms, how it would take hold of her imagination when she had hours ahead of her to calculate all the terrifying possibilities one by one. She had experienced it in Leipzig hundreds of times, in Berlin, in Paris. Feeling it each time she remembered her family or had no idea where she was. But what she sensed had happened to her on the plane was something different. Something immediate and clean. A kind of vertigo that was useless to rebel against.

Capa lit a cigarette and shook his head, softly trying to warn her, his expression serious, his tone paternalistic.

"Fear isn't a bad travel companion," he said, unaware that he was giving her the best advice you could give someone in a war. "Sometimes, it saves your life."

Barcelona was no longer the bourgeois and stately city Capa had visited many years ago during his first trip to Spain in the spring of 1935. The anarchist union of the Confederación Nacional del Trabajo (CNT) had built its provisional camp right on Vía Layetana, while many churches had become garages or warehouses, and the parish churches had been moved to union offices. The main banks and grand hotels had been taken over by the workers. The Partido Obrero de Unificación Marxista (POUM), with its Trotskyist tendencies, was based at the Hotel Falcon, close to the Plaça de Catalunya, while the Ritz was now a popular dining hall with a sign at its entrance that read: UGT–HOTEL GASTRÓNOMICO NÚMERO 1–CNT.

The commissioner of propaganda for the Generalitat de Catalunya, Jaume Miravitlles, was a tanned, affable man in his thirties, who provided them with a boardinghouse to stay in along La Rambla and the press passes necessary for photographing the city.

After the accident, the elation they felt being alive translated itself into their body language. It was as if they were celebrating every minute of being together in light of what could come. It showed in the way they made love, holding on to each other tightly, because one day in the near future one of them or both of them could die, and then there would be nothing, not a damn straw to clutch at. The amusing foreshortening of her lying across the bed with his pajamas on, tender and half-asleep. The good morning fights they had still half-asleep, over a sponge or because they lived together inside a small rectangle of a mirror. He, with half his face full of foam, trying to shave over her shoulder. She, trying to nudge him out with her elbows so she could put on her lipstick. Gerda's strange green eyes looking at him mockingly, halfway between coquettish and innocent.

The first few days, they walked the streets fascinated, among a multitude of armed men, children playing within the sandbags of the barricades, the militia dressed in blue uniforms with straps across their chests, from the CNT, the POUM, the PSUC. Female soldiers with black eyes and the tawny leonine manes, a newspaper in one hand and a Mauser in the other. Images that broke the traditional female codes of conduct; those women were another ilk. They weren't the type to hide their heads under the pillow when the coyote howled but would lean out the window and shoot, scaring away the Fascists in one clean shot. The French and British magazines went head-to-head to feature them on their covers, not only for their courage but because they imagined these women to be an iconographic goldmine. "The Glamour of War," Capa declared with a wry grin, while a confiscated car with the acronym of the UHP painted onto its doors cruised down the Paseo de Gracia at full speed toward Capitania.

In just a few days, they were moving around that town as if they'd been raised in the neighborhood of Gracia. They combed the city bit by bit, living off every scrap of emotion, trying to interpret the world with their cameras. However, all of the photos were copyrighted by "Capa," and in the beginning it was especially easy to distinguish whose work it was. He worked with a quick-shot Leica that could easily get up close to his subject. His frames tended to be tighter than hers, but they almost always included other elements that gave them a special life. Gerda used a Rolleiflex that she hung over her chest and that was slower. She took her time preparing a frame. From a technical point of view, her photographs were better executed but more conventional. She lacked spontaneity. As a beginner, she still wasn't sure of herself. But she had the intuition to identify irreproducible moments. A couple sits in the sun. The man is wearing the militia's hat and blue uniform and is holding a rifle that's resting on the ground. The woman is very blond and wears a black dress. They are sharing a big laugh. Something about the couple drew Gerda's attention. Perhaps it was because they looked like her and Capa. Similar age, certain physical characteristics that were interchangeable, the same intimacy, that air of coconspirators. She focused. Positioning herself in contrast to the light, she searched for a frontal frame. Their two silhouettes cropped against a background of trees. Click. At first glance, it was a happy photograph, though there was a tragic halo over it, something vaguely premonitory about it.

But that wasn't anything close to real war. Below a stained-glass ceiling, thousands of soldiers thronged the Francia Station, prepared to head off to the Aragón Front, while the Union Radio's microphones continuously aired recruitment calls. Gerda and Capa photographed hundreds of young men saying good-bye to their girlfriends, grown men hugging their little ones, upright ladies urging them to hurry while helping them tuck their shirts into their pants correctly. There weren't any tears or Andromaches on that platform. Below the transversing morning light, there was only a dense railway vapor. Train cars with their doors open, filled with volunteers whose backs were covered with slogans written in white paint, such as BETTER DEAD THAN TYRANT LED. Young people full of vitality, sticking their heads out the window with their fists in the air. They had no idea what was waiting for them. The majority never saw Barcelona again.

In the Port of Cádiz, a freighter had just docked with the first shipment of Nazi ground troops and aircraft on Spanish soil.

Chapter Thirteen

A narrow highway. The light from the sun staining the roof of the car. A lit cigarette, an elbow resting over a rolled-down window. Capa was driving with caution, due to all the curves and consecutive checkpoints, Gerda leaning back in her seat, the arid wind of the olive groves blowing through her hair. She was whistling the tune of a song that could be heard everywhere in those days.

> *I climbed up a green pine tree*
> *To see if . . . and I saw*
> *To see if . . . and I saw.*
> *And I only saw an armored train*
> *Its guns . . . blasting away. . .*
> *Its guns . . . blasting away.*
> *Come on shout, shout!*
> *The engine hisses*
> *As Franco . . . passes by*
> *As Franco . . . passes by*

Riding in an official press vehicle, Gerda and Capa traveled along the same highway that the motorized columns were using to get to the front. Her knee was on the gearbox, bumping up against it every time they hit a pothole. She enjoyed the closeness they had in that car while traveling over a land they hardly knew and didn't love yet. Along the way, they came upon several trucks with the flying red-and-black flags of the CNT. They'd rumble every now and again, like faraway thunder or the roar of a missile.

They had set up the front in Huesca. Everything moved at such a slow pace that the militia, after positioning their machine guns into place, still had enough time to help the local farmers in the surrounding areas with their crops and threshing wheat. Gerda would walk silently through the yellow fields with mountains of straw on the edges of their paths, photographing all the agricultural hard work around her as part of the overall defense of the Republic. But so much tranquility drove Capa crazy. The only thing he wanted to do was photograph a Republican victory already.

They traveled several miles toward the southeast, where they'd been told the Thälmann Battalion was operating from. For the most part, it was made up of volunteers from the Communist Party, who were mostly Polish and German Jews. The battalion was a creation of the International Brigades. A majority had traveled to Barcelona in order to participate in the Workers' Olympiad, an alternative to the Berlin Olympics, but the Olympiad had been suspended because of the war. Gerda and Capa thought it was a good opportunity for someone who spoke their language to bring them up to date on how things were going. The Spanish they spoke was limited to a few key phrases, and they tried following conversations without understanding a damn thing. But at least they were entertained by all the gesticulations and verbal outbursts. *Salud. Camarada. Por los cojones.* That was their basic vocabulary for getting by in that godforsaken land.

When they arrived to Leciñena, some twelve miles from Zaragoza, they came upon a group of combatants in helmets and espadrilles reading *Arbeiter-Illustrierte Zeitung.* The town was the center of operations for the POUM column, and one that George Orwell would pass through the following winter, before he was injured. It was a relief to be able to exchange impressions regarding the latest encouraging news from Madrid with them: an armed *pueblo*, the people, marching through Alcalá and Toledo, and resistance in Asturias . . . But it also seemed they weren't going to find the action they were seeking there, either. The settlement had been achieved through a nighttime surprise attack, but since then, very few confrontations had been registered, and the soldiers limited themselves to awaiting word, bored and having to endure a scorching heat that tried the nerves of even the most resistant. Capa couldn't take anymore. Those dead hours weighed on his shoulders like lead.

Using his foot, he pushed open a garage-type door that led down a hallway to an old grocery warehouse converted into a makeshift tavern. Below the strings of garlic hanging from the ceilings, and in front of a billboard for Heno de Pravia soap, every afternoon the sweaty, bare-chested soldiers would kill time skillfully emptying wineskins in the Aragón tradition.

"We don't serve alcohol to women," said the bartender—a short and stout man in civilian dress—when he saw Gerda, with her elbows on the bar, casually smoking Gauloises Bleues.

"Can't you see she's a foreigner?" blurted out one of the seated POUM men from a nearby table. "If the Fascists can shoot her, then that means you can serve her red wine as well, *coño*."

But before she and Capa were able to realize the motive behind the argument, the bartender had already climbed up onto a platform to fill a wineskin.

"International press," said the corporal who had joined them, introducing himself to the pair.

Before such a show of foreign allegiance and professionalism, the poor bartender didn't know how to apologize. He dried his hands on his apron and planted a bottle of red wine along with two chipped cups on the bar for them.

"You'll have to pardon me, but the glasses end up breaking and since we're no longer manufacturing them . . ."

"It doesn't matter, Paco. Don't get overly refined on us now," said the corporal. "They're trustworthy."

However, the argument was still lingering in the air. Despite images of militiawomen with rifles sitting in cafés, the Communists were in favor of relegating their participation to the rearguard, and for the Republicans, the debate not only poisoned their words but divided them. In fact, only a month later, in the fall, the minister of war, Largo Caballero, prohibited militiawomen from being on the frontlines and would take away their uniforms if they disobeyed.

"The bartender is right," declared a volunteer from the Thälmann Battalion in German. He was a thin Communist who wore glasses and was an expert in logistics. "You bring your women to this war as if you were here on vacation. You have to be fucking kidding, getting them involved in this mess. If they want to help, they should work as nurses at the hospitals, like the colored women in North America, where there are plenty of bandages that need trimming."

It was just what Capa needed to release all that tension built up during his idle time. He turned to the man with the look of one possessed son of a bitch, his muscles tense, his arms slightly raised off his body.

"And who gave you the right to butt into this conversation?" he asked. "Did someone ask your opinion? Did I perhaps mention your girlfriend waiting for you back home playing the piano and making strawberry jam? Well, now you know some women prefer to take photographs so the entire world can see what's happening in this country, and if you don't like it, you're screwed."

"We'll see who's screwed when they put a bullet in her or when they fire at you because of her. You'll see, in certain situations women are no more than trouble."

Feeling a bit uncomfortable, Gerda followed the argument without wanting to intervene. If there were men still living in the last century, it was them, even if they were Communists.

"If they put a bullet in me, it's my problem," said Capa, staring at him with a very serious look on his face. "No one else's. She's risking herself like I am. So, she goes where I go. And if her presence bothers you, you already know where the door is." Capa pointed to the jute cloth hanging over the archway leading to the back room.

Gerda smiled at him. It was moments like this that made her love that proud Hungarian with his devilish character and lack of manners. Maybe on some occasions he was overly egotistical and ambitious, getting hotheaded over stupidities, like anyone else. But you could trust him and he had a burning temper that caused him to behave with more audacity than most men would in the same situation. Noble, somewhat cocky, and painfully handsome, she thought to herself, trying to secure him in her memory just as he was in that moment: his shirt open, his facial expression harsh, his fists clenched in his pockets, swearing at the German and the mother who gave birth to him.

"Beauty draws more than five yoke of oxen," said a local civilian, who, despite not speaking languages, and as drunk as he was, understood immediately what the fight was about.

The German quietly placed his glasses in a cup and polished off his drink in one gulp. Hopefully those Nationalists will give you hell and you'll have to swallow your words, you idiot, was what he was probably thinking, though he didn't say a word.

However, it was he who'd have to swallow them, one by one, only a short while after. On the twenty-fifth of the month, just a few miles away, in Tardienta, shrapnel would fly into his leg when his battalion tried blowing up a Francoist train carrying ammunition and a young English volunteer named Felicia Browne would rescue him off the train tracks. She dragged him by the shoulders for twenty-five yards until she could find a safe shelter for him behind an embankment, risking her life during the Fascist crossfire. But when she turned back to rejoin her comrades, one of Franco's legionnaires blew her breastbone to pieces with a submachine gun. Thirty-two years old. Painter. Woman. The first British casualty. There are men who need indisputable evidence to fall from their high horse. Others never can.

He had a point, thought Capa. The incident only helped reinforce something he had already learned about the country on his first visit. When you're dealing with Spaniards, their rules of conduct are clear and impossible to confuse. You have to offer the men tobacco and leave the women alone.

What could those arid plains that transmitted a suffocating sense of solitude mean for a pair of young photographers like them? Especially when contemplated beneath a motionless sky and through a camera's viewfinder? At that point, they probably still weren't sure what territory they had set foot on, but had begun to feel an affection toward it anyway. Mostly inspired by the admiration they had for its people's austere order, their brash sense of humor, and the *pueblo*'s fierce determination to keep their feet firm on the ground. They both wanted to become a part of that scenery. And like that river that traverses countless countries along its course, they slowly began letting go of their origins. Wanting to remove the shackles of their respective homelands. That was the first lesson that Spain taught them. Sun and olive trees. Nations do not exist. Only the *pueblos* exist.

At sunset, they strolled through the plaza, past walls plastered with last season's yellowing bullfighting posters. Stopping to photograph the militia listening to a speech by Manuel Grossi, the leader of Asturia's miners union, being given from the balcony of the town hall. Then sat down to drink from a bottle that someone had offered them from their doorstep while the bell tower rang seven times, its cement base still standing despite being eaten away by mortar shrapnel. Then, as if they were in the middle of the desert, they heard the faraway tinkling of a herd of goats returning home. The heat and distance distorted their images into undulating mirages. In fact, the POUM's headquarters looked like a Bedouin camp, the strings of their tents securely tied. The news of Federico García Lorca's assassination in Granada reached them one evening. That was the other face of Spain, the one that burned books and screamed: "Down with intelligence!" "Long live death!" The one that hated thinking and shot their best poet at daybreak.

Gerda and Capa spoke little during those walks. As if each needed to react on their own while facing that land inhabited by skinny dogs and old women dressed in black, their faces chiseled by strong winds, weaving wicker baskets under the shade of a fig tree. Gerda began to realize that perhaps the real face of the war wasn't just the price paid for the blood and disemboweled bodies that she would soon see but the bitter wisdom that lived in those women's eyes, a dog's solitude as it wandered through the fields limping, a hind leg broken by a bullet. The horror inside a wooden drawer containing a small bundle wrapped in cloth, about the size of a two-pound bag of rice. She was training her photographer's eye, and little by little, she was developing an extraordinary talent for observation. Curious, she lifted the tip of the cloth with caution and discovered the dead body of a few-months-old baby dressed in a white shirt with lace trimming, whose parents were planning to bury their child that very afternoon. She kept quiet but went out walking by herself until she reached the edge of an embankment and sat down. Resting her head on her knees, she began to cry, hard and long, with tears that dripped onto her pants, unable to control herself, without really knowing why she was crying, completely alone, staring out into that horizon of yellow countryside. She had just learned her first important lesson as a journalist. No scenery could ever be as devastating as a human story. This would be her photography's signature. The snapshots she captured with her camera those days were not the images of war that militant magazines such as *Vu* or *Regards* awaited. But those slightly inclined frames transmitted a greater sense of sadness and loneliness than the war itself. A low sky, soldiers along a highway, small clouds of smoke in the distance.

At night they all sat around a campfire. For dinner, they cooked rabbit in a dark, red wine sauce, garnished with green peppers and chickpeas. It was well prepared, but she couldn't eat a bite. Her head was somewhere else. That's why when Capa proposed they continue on the road to Madrid the next morning, she felt as though he had cut the invisible cords that were keeping her from breathing.

"Let's go," she said.

Chapter Fourteen

Madrid, heart of Spain,
beats with a fever's pulse;
if its blood boiled yesterday
it boils with more fury today . . .

The verses of Rafael Alberti sounded at all hours of the day on Radio Madrid. The city had already undergone two bombings, and although the Loyalist troops were able to detain the Fascists' advancement through the Sierra of Guadarrama, there was further alarming news regarding a large Francoist contingency approaching from the southeast. The city prepared for the worst. It was on Calle San Bernardo, in front of the streetcar depot, where Capa heard for the second time a group of militia shouting the cry of Pétain in Verdun: "*Ils ne passeront pa*s." This time a little louder, and in Spanish: *NO PASARÁN. They shall not pass.* Wars also leave behind them a wealth of phrases that link one caste's blood to another. It's happened since the days of Troy. Unique to war is its ability to reverse time.

Entire villages put to the sword, women raped and skinned to nothing, houses in flames. Waterloo, Verdun, the Inquisition's stakes, Goya's *Disasters*, Dos de Mayo . . .

The sensation of being in a city under attack was much more evident than what Gerda and Capa had experienced in Barcelona. In Madrid, the neon lights were kept low and one had to keep their windows closed. When the sirens sounded, the entire electric current was interrupted. Nonetheless, the capital believed in itself and continued dreaming in its own manner. That's what Gerda loved about it. *Madrileños* also liked going to the movies. Lining up for Fred Astaire and Ginger Rogers, though on the way home they'd have to throw themselves on the floor of their streetcars in case a bullet came through. The women would stand there mesmerized by the couple in the movie poster that included a tiny frieze of American skyscrapers in the background. He, thin and tapping in tails. She, smiling and with those transparent eyes of a working-class girl who's arrived. A tad naive, gullible like all women, watching him twirl around her like an angel with wings. After the movie, those same dreaming women would head to the fronts in Guadarrama or Ciudad Universitaria to fire their guns, while a large part of those ticket-holders would end up supplying the hospitals with enough blood on hand. Tap dancing was a way of blocking out the hammering of the machine guns arriving from across the border. While Capa was lost driving along Calle de Quevedo, looking for the Hotel Florida, Gerda stuck her camera out the window. Outside the entrance to the Proyecciones movie house, two dark-haired children with dirty knees were dancing on the asphalt. They'd stuck tacks on the tips and the heels of their shoes so they could imitate Fred Astaire. An acacia branch used for a cane, an invisible top hat. In the midst of all that hunger and fear, a graceful elegance had blossomed, like the world from the other side of the mirror. Click.

Madrid was that. Golden skies before the battle. The workers placing a domed wall of bricks around Cibeles to protect it.

They were stretched out on their hotel bed, completely nude. Rays of light filtering through the blinds. Their eyes staring at the ceiling.

"Do you ever think to yourself that it can all just end one day?" asked Gerda. She spoke with a certain vagueness, her arms crossed and tucked under her head.

"What can? This?"

"Yes . . . I don't know." She remained silent as if she was thinking about something that was hard to express. "Everything."

It was the kind of observation that would cause Capa's head to pound. Not because of its meaning, but for what he didn't understand about her. When she said those things, he felt as if only her body was close to his. He turned over to look at her, like that, so thin, with her clavicle pressing up against her skin like a small chicken wing, her ribs aligned just like a ship's logbook.

"You women are complicated," he said, gliding the palm of his hand over her stomach, still smelling of semen.

"Why?"

"I don't know, Gerda, sometimes you can appear like a little girl and I enjoy watching you walk down the street with your hands in your pockets, swaying your hips a little, smiling . . ."

"You only like my hips?"

"No. I also like seeing you stick half your body out the window like you did this afternoon, taking shots of those children dancing in the streets. And I like that little space you have between your teeth," he said, opening her mouth with one of his fingers. "I like all of you, even the pornography. And I love when you throw your head back when you roar with laughter. Or when you decide to cook something and there's nobody who wants to eat it."

"Oh come on now, I'm not that bad," she joked, hitting him in the face with a pillow.

"And I especially like you when you're sitting in Maria Eisner's office, and, in a very serious tone, you let out a 'That Capa bastard took off again with some actress to the Côte d'Azur. Damn him.'" He imitated her voice and mannerisms to perfection.

Now both of them were laughing. The black clouds had passed

again. Capa reached over to the night table to grab the cigarettes.

"And I don't like you at all, and I mean at all, at other times," he said, placing a lit cigarette in her mouth.

"Which times?"

"Well, when you start saying strange things about being a German or Polish Jew, or whatever you are, in such a serious way that you frighten me, with that crease you get there, between your eyebrows, and with such a long face you look like Kierkegaard."

"That awful?" she complained.

"Worse than awful, a hideous insect from hell," he said, taking her head into his hands and lowering himself onto her, noticing how hard his sex was again. He slowly opened her thighs with his fingers so he could sink inside of her again, his breath faltering, trapping her in his arms, licking her chin, her clavicle bone, her ribs, one by one. "But I know the secret for making you beautiful again, like the princess in the stories," he said, lowering himself slowly toward the concave slope of her stomach. Her mound curly and warm, beating like the heart of a wound within the shadow of her pubis. He separated her legs a little more, stroking her ankles, the smooth skin of her thighs, leaving a trail of saliva behind on her skin. Then, slowly heading higher and higher, he carefully spread her mound open, determined, lowering his mouth onto it, slow and deep, just as he would kiss her mouth, turning away slightly to catch his breath or remove a hair from his lips, delicate, brooding, his face moist, while she softly pushed his head lower, going beyond the offering or the shame, right before it all started again. The shortness of breath, the last of the sunlight through the gaps in the blinds, the sensation that you're about to fall at any minute, and as she held on to his back and abandoned herself to that last unconscious pleasure, it suddenly occurred to her that this surely couldn't last.

But she didn't feel sadness or fear. Just a strange feeling of melancholy, as if from that exact point forward she would no longer care if she died.

A dark hotel room. A topographical map. An open travel bag. Two cameras on the night table and, every so often, the flash of an explosion in the Sierra de Guadarrama.

Capa was smoking a cigarette now and peeking out the window, going against regulations. A blinded Madrid, without electricity.

Two months later, she'd remember that cigarette, when the war wasn't like it was now, an orange flash at nightfall but a shower of iron that intensified everywhere. Bullets, shards, and artillery shells ricocheting off the walls, *fsssiaaang, fsssiaaang* . . . Avenida del Quince y Medio was what the *Madrileños* called the Gran Vía in those days, a reference to the shells that were habitually dropped, delivered with their traditionally biting humor. By that point, the entire city was one big trench full of holes, where even the tobacco was rationed and all there was to eat was oatmeal and sweet potato. Tap, tap, tap, tap . . . The sound of Fred Astaire's light and nimble tapping had been converted into a deafening rattle, mixed with sirens wailing, while people rushed down stairwells to get to the underground shelters, and howitzers opened fire on the Telefónica building itself. But not yet. Now they were nude by the window, holding each other close, looking out into the night. Gerda could see how Capa had wrinkled up his eyebrows rushing through the last drag of his cigarette. The shadow of his beard adding a look of obstinacy to his face. She knew him well enough to know what he was thinking. He was worried that he still hadn't taken one single shot that was worth something.

"We have to get closer," he said.

"I agree."

"We only have two options," he said as he unfolded the map before her, illuminating it with a flashlight. "Toledo or Córdoba."

In Toledo, the seditious General Moscardó had taken over the city by enclosing himself within a castle-fortress with close to a thousand allied soldiers, along with their families, women, and children, in addition to having taken more than a hundred captives that included Leftists from the vicinity. The Republican forces had spent weeks besieging the Alcázar without success. It was an impregnable fortress. It was said that a group of Asturian dynamite experts from the carbon mines were excavating two tunnels where they planned to deposit explosives under its walls in order to create an opening.

In Córdoba, the Republican government had launched a major offensive to reclaim the city from the clutches of General Varela. The authorities announced new advances every day, and the need for a victory had caused the false rumor that Loyalist troops had been able to enter the city to start circulating. After evaluating the situation carefully, Gerda and Capa arrived at the conclusion that the dynamite experts probably still had a ways to go in the tunnels.

They chose Córdoba.

The most important photo of his life was waiting for him there, though Capa didn't know it. It was an image that would make him famous, that would circulate the world's major magazine covers and convert him into an authentic twentieth-century icon. It was a photograph that would cause him to instantly feel a radical and profound hate for his occupation and perhaps for himself as well. For all that he stopped being from that moment on: a Hungarian boy who was raised in Pest, who could never go back to being a twenty-two-year-old.

There were still three long years of war left to fight in Spain, an extended seven more during the world war, and a few more for its consequences: Palestine, Korea, Indochina . . . and plenty more nights filled with boredom and despair, leaning out the window of any hotel in the world. Remembering.

Wars are full of people who can only look back. Because sometimes life twists itself so much that one is left to sort it out however they can.

That night, the journalist Clemente Cimorra, a correspondent for the Madrid daily *La Voz*, walked into the Bar Chicote on Gran

Vía with mountains of sandbags out in front to protect its large windows. Cimorra had one earphone plugged in and the other hanging below his chin. A journalist from the *Herald Tribune* had given him the latest crystal radio, and he went everywhere with it. In part, he was being pretentious, while the other part was about being on top of the latest news.

The bar's loyal clientele—made up of militia, writers, foreign correspondents, and the International Brigade with their leather jackets and "blond cigarettes," female companions wearing fake pearls and the old-fashioned kind of rice powder on their faces—had arrived at the bar with the modernist decór and world-renowned cocktails to eventually all gather around the veteran journalist and anxiously await a verdict.

"Those damn Frenchies!" he spat.

The breaking news reported that France's government had refused to supply arms to the Republic. No one had expected anything from Great Britain, but the French were their next-door neighbors, a sister government to the Popular Front. Everyone still recalled the words of Dolores Ibárruri, a woman raised in the mines of the Basque lands. At the last Communist meeting held in Paris's Vélodrome d'Hiver, she had spoken up in her deep voice of a miner's wife and daughter, and said: "You must help the Spanish people. Today it's us, but your turn will come tomorrow. We need rifles and canons in order to defeat the Fascism on our common borders."

They decided not to listen to her.

Chapter Fifteen

Deserted roads. Abandoned homes. Windows barred and doors bolted shut. Herds of stray cows wandering aimlessly through the streets. A ghost town. The type of place where common sense would tell you to stop the car and head back the other way.

They had left Madrid at the break of dawn, well prepared with their press identifications and documents of safe conduct, heading to the Republican headquarters in Montoro, not far from Córdoba, which took them three days by car. From there they continued onto Cerro Muriano. The day smelled of molasses, with a lukewarm sun that stewed the walls of the houses and the blood on the geraniums that decorated the balconies. It was one of those days when the war machinery stops for a few minutes before it starts up again at full force. Gerda and Capa also stopped to drink water from the fountain, taking advantage of the respite to sit down on a doorstep and ask themselves what the hell had happened there that there was no one left. There weren't any signs of violence. No broken windows. No burned crops. But in the plaza, the only thing you could hear were the disoriented bells of the goats. Everyone had fled. Men, women, and children. By foot, on the backs of mules, by car . . .

Only a few hours before, the insurgent general Queipo de Llano had sworn over the radio that his men would soon be arriving to declare their right to *droit de seigneur*.

People believe that the most devastating part of a war are the corpses with their guts out in the open, the puddles of blood, and all that you can capture at first glance. But sometimes the horror is off to the side, in the lost look on the face of a woman who's just been raped, as she limps away alone within the ruins, trying to keep her head down. Gerda and Capa were not aware of this yet. They were too young. And that was their first conflict. They still believed war had its romantic side.

First thing in the morning, the German reporters Hans Namuth and Georg Reisner, who also contributed content to *Vu* magazine and Alliance Photo, along with the Austrian journalist Franz Borkenau, had managed to photograph the terrified exodus of Cerro Muriano's inhabitants under a sky filled with Francoist planes while Queipo de Llano continued to harass women over the radio. There was nothing that ticked Capa off more than arriving at places after others had already been there. But during wartime, it's never clear what came before or what came after.

They left their car in the town and continued walking along the highway, following the indications on the map to the place where they had been told a militiawoman from the CNT was camping out. Along the way, they took photographs of the last villagers that had lagged behind. Silent faces, women carrying their children in their arms, elderly couples with bloodshot eyes, constantly looking back. The look that Lot's wife wore before she turned into a pillar of salt. People who flee.

Capa observed Gerda walking silently on the other side of the highway. She didn't look back. Her camera on top of her chest, her hair falling over her forehead, short, very blond, burned by the sun, a gray shirt, her skinny legs sheathed in a pair of canvas pants tucked inside her military boots, the highway's gravel crunching below her footsteps. So agile and slight, from behind she looked like a boy-soldier. Capa had seen her stop at the side of a ditch, looking all around her with the caution of a clever hunter, making her calculations, mentally preparing the photo. As they started getting closer to the front, she quickened her pace, as if she were late for an appointment. He was also making his own calculations, and according to his numbers, her period was already a week late compared to when it had arrived the month before.

Since the forced landing in Barcelona, she appeared quieter, closed off, as if something had really happened to her or she had suddenly understood that prodigious characteristic that certain places can have to transform people within. She was constantly reading everything that had to do with Spain's history, its customs and geography . . . She was discovering the country at the same time she was discovering herself. Capa noticed her self-education process as well, seeing her change a little every day; her determined chin, her defined cheekbones, her eyes more translucent, like grapes within the light of the harvest, secretive, protecting something inside. Deep in her gaze, he feared the subtle changes that had occurred that didn't involve him. He believed women had a much greater capacity for transformation than men did, and that was what, in his gut, he feared most: that those changes could wind up with her distancing herself from him. She didn't need him anymore, no longer asking his advice as she did in the beginning. Even the photographs she took had begun emancipating themselves from him, acquiring their own approach. She always moved in relation to things, exploring their limits, the profile of a jaw, the plummeting edges of a precipice . . . More autonomous every day, more in charge of her actions. It was then that Capa knew, with the dry certainty of a revelation, that he would not be able to live without her.

They arrived at the top of Las Malagueñas hill by noon. During the next few days, the CNT militia had planned to launch an attack on the city of Córdoba, located eight miles to the south.

However, they were completely disorganized. There was no chain of command. Their soldiers looked like fresh recruits with more courage than military training. A small group of militia from Alcoy fraternized with the journalists who had arrived to cover the attack in a relaxed atmosphere, playing cards and drinking with enthusiasm.

"The worst part of the war is tolerating the tedium of waiting, guy," a veteran journalist said to him upon seeing the look of deception on his face. It was Clemente Cimorra, the *La Voz* correspondent whom they both had met at the Chicote, though now he wasn't carrying his transistor radio attached to his ear.

But they didn't have to wait long. A few minutes later, the combatants were ready to go. It was the first scuffle they'd witness from such a close distance. The group was made up of a few journalists and fifty militiamen, whose mission was to defend Murcia's artillery regiment located behind the front line of Alcoy's infantry column. Capa insisted that Gerda not remain on the hill.

"Too dangerous," he said, as if it had already been decided.

"Don't start with that now," she said, looking offended. "We've already discussed this several times."

She had gotten up to look for the lighter in her pants pocket and raised a rolled, filterless cigarette to her mouth.

Capa just stood looking at her with the same hardened expression, not allowing his arm to be twisted.

"No way."

"And who do you think you are? My father? My brother? My babysitter? Or what?" Now she was looking him straight in the face, defiant, her eyes shining with fire.

"I don't want anything to happen to you," he said, this time in a conciliatory tone, and then added, with that half-smile of his that was part ironic, part gentle, "It's not that I really care that much— it's just that I don't want to be left without a manager."

"Well, you'll have to get used to it."

It sounded like the threat it was. Capa looked away. She was fast with her comebacks and she wasn't the type to allow herself to be taken advantage of by anyone. Then he observed her for a minute and a half without opening his mouth. Resolute, firm, bold, able to drive him mad like no one else.

"Fine," he said. "You're on your own." He loved that skinny Jew, obstinate, egotistical, and unbearable. He loved her through and through.

They began walking behind the column, over the ochre-colored stubble, past splashes of stones and trees amputated by the recent attack of pack howitzers, heading to the hill's summit. In the distance, they could see the bluish crest of the Sierra. Capa walked, trying to maintain a bit of space between them to see if she could manage on the uneven terrain. When he offered his hand to help her climb a rock, she refused it.

"I can do it alone," she said with that characteristic impulse of her personality.

He watched her out of the corner of his eye, climbing the steepest part of the hill, without opening her mouth. Not one complaint, not one comment; silent, shooting glances at her surroundings in between photographs.

"Do exactly what I do. Stay close behind me. Keep your eyes on the terrain. Always look for a protective slope. You have to hop along, in stages." Capa gave her instructions without looking at her, as if talking to himself in a tone that was harsh and surly, ill-tempered. "And never raise your camera to the sun when there are planes flying close by, dammit!"

"Cerro Muriano, September 5, 1936. Two very young kids . . . practically two children," wrote Clemente Cimorra in his daily chronicle, converting the two into the day's protagonists without them knowing it. "With nothing in their hands but their photo cameras, a Leica and a Rolleiflex. They spy the movements of a plane that tilts its wings vertically over their heads. He and she, these two kids who now accompany me, are able to take photographs of the very flame of the event. They drag themselves through the areas that have been worst hit by gunfire . . . This kind of intrepid journalism isn't a myth, believe me. It's the bravery of generous youth who seek to document [history]. They're one of us. *Gauche divine* people . . . [The Divine Left]."

The attack was interrupted somewhere between the hours of one and three in the afternoon. They took advantage of the free time and went to rest at the camp's base. As they sat together, Capa wouldn't take his eyes off Gerda. Her shapely chest under that gray shirt caused him to suddenly feel a strong pang in his groin. It had begun to happen to him more frequently. As if the risks they were taking had fully awakened his physical reflexes, like the ones he used when he hid behind a slope, no different from the desire he had to hold her tight now. Because he never knew when his time would come. Like the French reporter for *L'Humanité*, Mario Arriette, who'd been gunned down on the Aragón front a few days after they had taken off from Leciñena. Or perhaps she'd be the one dead, and then he wouldn't be able to handle it, and he'd die of anguish and despair and guilt and he wouldn't be able to forgive himself for not giving her a good slap on the face while there was still time. It was what he longed to do the entire day. In the blink of an eye, a clean and neat slap on the face, nothing more. So she'd listen to reason. Because it was one thing was to cover the rearguard of the war, and he never gave her any trouble about that. And another thing was being on the front lines, which was very different. Throwing yourself into the open field, dragging yourself facedown on the ground so you can pass under the bullets, up to your ears covered in dirt, trying to advance with great difficulty to the next stone wall to try and see what was happening on the other side. But there she was, with the look of someone with few friends, frowning, scratches on her forehead, dirt on her pants, more distant than ever, certain she was right, with Kierkegaard's crease between her brows, and the only thing that he could think of was kissing her until that hard line disappeared from her face. He couldn't help it. It was impossible to bear a grudge for even a second when she was in his presence. He wanted to squeeze her tight in his arms, make her forget all those impertinent words they'd said and all the ones they were capable of saying. Because the only thing that mattered in the end was that need of physical contact before battle. Without uttering a word, he cleaned his knife with a piece of bread and placed it back into his pocket. Lead on the horizon.

By the late afternoon, each of them went their own way. Capa decided to stay with the Alcoy militia in a trench by the hill, suspecting he'd have a better chance of taking the action shot he wanted over there. She preferred to travel a few kilometers more with the rest of the journalists, to be there just in case the advance party with Republican artillery launched their attack against General Varela's troops in their barracks. Among the foreign journalists was a nineteen-year-old Canadian named Ted Allan, with whom she got along well, who was shy, long-legged, light-eyed, and who looked a bit like Gary Cooper in *The Lives of a Bengal Lancer.*

He was the first to hear the faraway blast on Las Malagueñas hill. Ta-ta-ta-ta-ta-ta . . . Followed by a hollow silence. Then a shorter burst, ta-ta-ta-ta . . . and more silence. They were in a valley and the surrounding terrain only magnified the sound.

"It's a Breda machine gun, Italian," he said. "And it looks like a crossfire."

He was young but had done his military service as a combat engineer and knew what he was talking about. He could detect where shots fired several miles away were coming from by the duration of their echo. Instinctively, he looked at his watch. Five o'clock in the afternoon. They all feared that the enemy troops had infiltrated the back of the Republican line and were shooting at them from behind, and applying a pincer maneuver on them from the front. The Alcoy militia were only equipped with Mauser rifles and light machine guns.

Gerda felt a sharp pain in her stomach. Everything had frozen in her interior, as if her blood and her heart were waiting in suspense. She had felt it before she began to reason with it, in fact, it was before she could mentally call upon her God: *Yahweh*, *Elohim*, *Adonai*, *Roi* . . . An instant reflex that couldn't be restrained by her own will, like putting up your arms to protect yourself from a blow. She remained still, looking from side to side, not knowing what to do. Pale. Confused. Her mouth was dry and her hands were like icicles. Her first instinct was to run toward the hill. But Ted grabbed her by the shoulders.

"Take it easy," he said. "We can't cross the field that way. In order to get back, we have to wait until it gets dark and cut through the town."

Gerda distanced herself a few paces in the direction of a large rock. She felt ill. She noticed she had a tight knot in the pit of her stomach; she held on to the rock and vomited everything she'd eaten.

Little by little, the blasts began to space themselves out. The waiting. The silence in the camps after combat. The dark sky. The somber silhouette of the sierra. She saw the first falling star from the grass, lying face-up as she did when she was a girl. Everything was so still around her it felt as though she were in a theatrical backdrop. Her friend was still at her side, quiet. The angel who remained silent.

They arrived at the camp when the sky was pitch-black, and at two hundred yards Gerda could already hear Capa's voice, though it sounded as dry as a dormant volcano, and she couldn't make out what he was saying. It turned out he was arguing with someone.

"Didn't you want a photo?" said the captain of the brigades. "Well, now you have your damn photo," he said, in a tone filled with more anger than disdain, the moment that Gerda, Ted, and everyone else arrived to their area of level ground. He was a well-built man, with solid arms, his skin weathered from being outdoors.

He stared at Capa deliberately. As if he didn't want to ever forget his face or was making an effort to contain himself and not break it with a punch.

Capa eyed him evasively, rubbing his neck in a way that showed his disconcertment, like the boxer who ignores the bell, knocked out, with barely enough motor skills to face the situation with fortitude. Undoubtedly, he'd been drinking. He could barely hold himself up, and he had a strange look on his face that Gerda had never seen before, somewhere between crestfallen and vexed, as if he had gone to a place of no return. His shirt was unbuttoned and hanging out of his pants, his hair disheveled. Gerda had never seen him like this. Not even when his father died.

"But what's all this about?" she wanted to know.

"Ask him," answered the captain.

Chapter Sixteen

A militiaman runs down the edge of a hill covered in weeds. The sleeves on his white shirt rolled up to his elbows, his soldier's cap thrown back, a rifle in his hand, and three leather cartridges fastened to a bandolier. The five-o'clock-in-the-afternoon sun casts its long shadow in the distance. One foot flying off the ground. His chest pushed out. Arms on a cross. A crucified Christ. Click.

Later on, in the red half-light of a Paris lavatory's darkroom, this man's face began to emerge from the bottom of the tray. His eyebrows bushy, his ears large, his forehead high, his chin tilted forward. The unknown militiaman.

The photograph was published in *Vu*, in a special September edition on the Spanish Civil War, and the following year in *Regards*, in *Paris-Soir*, and in a special edition of *Life*, with a caption that explained how Robert Capa's camera caught a Spanish soldier the instant he is dropped by a bullet through the head on the Córdoba front. The image caused a sensation throughout the world due to its visceral perfection. Hundreds of shaken-up readers mailed letters to their newspapers. No European or North American middle-class home had ever seen an image like that.

"Death of a Loyalist Militiaman" contained all of the drama of Goya's *Third of May 1808* painting, all the rage that *Guernica* would later show, all the mystery that strangles the soul of men and obligates them to fight knowing what they're fighting for. The danger, the melancholy, the infinite solitude, the broken dreams. The very moment of death on an abandoned Spanish plain. Its strength, like all symbols, didn't lie in just the image but in what it was representing.

And who can remain impartial before barbarism? How does one pass through the dead with their eyes shut and their boots clean? How can one not take sides? There are photos that are meant not for remembering but for comprehending. Images that become symbols of an era, although no photographer is aware of this when taking them. A man is firing his gun while leaning up against a slope of a ditch; he hears the blast of machine-gun fire; he lifts his camera without even looking. The rest is a mystery. "The prize picture is born in the imagination of editors and [the] public who sees them," said Capa before a microphone of New York's WNBC radio station almost ten years later, when Gerda was already within the black outer limits of ether. And she listened to him millions of light-years away, out on the balcony of her star.

"One time I also shot a photo that was a lot more valued than the rest. And when I shot it, of course, I didn't know it was special. It was in Spain. At the very start of my career as a photographer. At the very start of the Civil War . . ."

People have always wanted to believe certain things about the nature of war. It's happened since the days of Troy. Heroism and tragedy, cruelty and fear, courage and defeat. All photographers hate those images that follow them like phantoms for the rest of their lives because of the mystery and scenic adversity it captures. Eddie Adams lived his entire life tormented by the snapshot he took in 1968, of a general from the Saigon police, at the precise moment he's firing point-blank at the temple of a Viet Cong prisoner with his hands tied behind his back. Due to the impact, the victim involuntarily tightens his face a second before his body begins to collapse. The photographer Nick Ut, from the Associated Press, could never forget the image of a nine-year-old Vietnamese girl burned by napalm, running naked on a road close to the small village of Trang Bang. In 1994, Kevin Carter took a photograph in Africa of an emaciated Sudanese child collapsed in an open field, less than a kilometer away from an ONU feeding center, while a vulture stalks her in the background. He won the Pulitzer for that photograph, and one month later he committed suicide. Robert Capa would never be able to overcome "Death of a Loyalist Militiaman"—the one they wound up calling "The Falling Soldier"—the best war photograph of all times.

Gerda was curled up on her side on top of the canvas blanket. She was facing in Capa's direction, with her left arm bent underneath her head as a pillow, her eyes open and fixed on him.

"Guess what time it is," she asked. It was a way, like any other, of breaking the ice.

"I don't know . . . is it still yesterday?"

She saw him pass a hand over his head, confused, sounding as if the alcohol's effluents still hadn't evaporated from his brain or as if he were talking in his sleep.

She touched his shoulder and remained with her eyes open within the darkness of the tent, contemplating the sparks of electricity on his jet-black hair.

"André . . ." she said in a low voice.

The name caught him by surprise. It had been a while since she last called him that. The warm tone stirred something inside of him. Without warning, he felt himself become fragile, like when he was a boy, sitting on the stairs of his house, petting the cat until the yelling subsided and he could tiptoe back to his room with a heavy heart.

"Yes?"

"What was it that happened?"

"I don't want to talk about it."

"It's best you do it now, André. It's not good to keep it inside. Did you ask the men to stage an attack?"

"No. We were just fooling around, that's all. Perhaps I complained that everything was far too calm and that there wasn't anything interesting to photograph. Then some of the men started to run down the slope and I joined in as well. We went up and down the hill several times. We were all feeling good. Laughing. They shot into the air. I took several photographs . . ." Capa remained still, his mouth had contorted itself, ". . . the damn photo."

"So what happened afterward?"

He remained silent far too many seconds for his pause to seem natural.

"What happened was that all of a sudden everything was real. We had a Francoist machine gun on the slope in front of us. Maybe we caught their attention with our voices. I didn't hear the shots . . . At first, I didn't hear them . . ." He looked at Gerda with his eyes fixed on hers, with loyalty and candidness, while at the same time on the defense.

That particular look she didn't have codified. And it caused her to feel a drop of fear, or, better yet, of apprehension. She didn't know how to interpret it. So she averted her eyes.

"That's enough. You don't have to go on if you don't want to." Suddenly, she remembered something that she also preferred to forget. "It's not necessary that you tell me, really. Don't tell me."

"You asked me. Now you must listen to me." There was no recrimination in Capa's voice, nor was there any mercy.

"Where were you?"

"A little farther ahead, off to the side, on a hill they call La Coja. The second burst of fire was shorter. One of the militiamen went to cover the other men's retreat and the machine gun opened fire. I raised my camera over my head and began to shoot as well." He didn't say anything for a few seconds, as if he were trying to fully analyze a thought that was difficult to grasp. To photograph people is to obligate them in some way to face things they weren't expecting to. You take them off their path, away from their plans, from their everyday routine. Sometimes it's also forcing them to die.

"It was nobody's fault, André. It happened. That's all," said Gerda, and just as she said it, the coincidence caused her to freeze. In Leipzig, Georg had used those exact words for the incident at the lake. The same words uttered in a low voice. John Reed's book on top of the linen tablecloth, the vase with tulips, and the pistol. She had never said a word about it to anyone.

"I did it automatically, without thinking," he continued. "When I saw him on the ground, I did not think he was dead. I thought he was faking it. That it was all a game. Then it turned silent. They all were looking at me. Two militiamen tried their best to drag him to the trench; another went to pick up his rifle and was shot in the act. That's when I realized what had happened. The Fascists had riddled him with bullets. But I killed him."

"It wasn't you, André," she consoled him, although, like him, deep down she knew if he hadn't been there with his camera, none of this would have happened.

"I'm not sure who he was. I've got the rattle of the machine-gun fire stuck here," he said, pointing to his forehead. "I don't even know his real name; he came as a volunteer from Alcoy with his little brother, who's about the same age as Cornell. I automatically pressed the camera's shutter release and he fell flat on his back, just as if I had fired a weapon that had reached his head. Cause and consequence."

"That's war, André."

Capa turned to face the wall. Gerda could not see his face. Just his back and his bare arms. As if he were trying to put a wall between them with that position. He was now on the other side of a collapsing bridge, where she could not get to him. He wasn't motionless or asleep. His back twitched in silence. The night's tremors on the body. Those who cry expend more energy doing that than with any other act. There were also things she was better off not thinking about. The sun had not yet risen. The blanket's dark canvas framed his body. At first, Gerda hesitated about whether or not to put her hand on his shoulder, ultimately deciding against it. There are times a man needs to fend for himself.

She remained on the other edge of the tent, covering his back from what was left of the night, without touching him. Calming him down when he awoke startled from a nightmare, until little by little the panic vanished, with Gerda at his side, her eyes wide open, also thinking in herself, of the solitude that penetrates your bones sometimes like an incurable illness, about the things that life shatters and that one cannot fix. That was the last time they'd ever discuss the photo. Nor did she ever call him André again.

Chapter Seventeen

The following morning, they set out for Madrid again. Gerda rolled down her window. She could hear the sound of the tires snapping over the arid land the entire way. She loved feeling the wind on her face: it helped her temporarily forget her need for a shower.

They arrived at Toledo at daybreak with kidneys aching from the potholes' constant jostling. September 18. A whitish light hovered over the olive groves, and in the distance, the massive silhouette of the Alcázar, bunker-like and impenetrable. They stopped to eat a breakfast of coffee and bread with olive oil at a roadway stand less than a kilometer away from the city. They needed to stretch their legs, smoke a cigarette. Words didn't come easy to Capa. He'd scratch his beard of several days and wrinkle up his entire face to think, as if trying to free himself of his thoughts, and only afterward could he say something. Gerda didn't look so good, either. She had her period and her stomach was in knots, along with a sharp pain she felt in her groin. Her shirt covered in several days' worth of dust, her hair greasy, her skin dry, trying to set up her camera, removing the lenses and cleaning them, one by one, with a look of complete concentration, the circles under her eyes accentuated by the clarity of the morning light.

A large group of photographers, journalists, news cameramen, and government officials arrived that same afternoon. From a nearby olive grove, they all awaited the destruction of the Alcázar's western wall. At six thirty, they heard a loud explosion. Five tons of dynamite. The black cloud of smoke covered the sun like an eclipse. A few minutes later, the fortress began to erupt like a volcano and its defenders gathered together on the opposite side to resist the sudden attack. Squashed together underneath a wall of pure rock were women and children, including a newborn baby named Restituto Valero, the son of a lieutenant from a band of Nationalists. The son of the Alcázar. After many years had passed—along with many battles, prisoners, and dead bodies—that child, now a captain of a paratrooper brigade, along with nine other of his armed comrades, would risk his hide and his career to defend democracy from the dictatorship of one General Franco, who had rescued him from the Alcázar while he was still in diapers. Paradoxes contain many cracks, and through one of them appeared a tiny head with live flesh and nerve endings. But none of this had happened yet. Back then, the baby's cries could be heard within the explosions, causing the hearts of the militia to shudder, because they were under strict orders to take over the fort however possible. Each time the militia poked their heads out from behind the wall's rubble, the insurgents would immediately attempt to drive them away. Gerda and Capa watched them climb that steep slope and fall almost instantly in the face of their gunfire. The wounded, dripping blood, were taken down in stretchers to the olive grove. They'd leave them there, lying face-up. Gerda kneeled down in a ditch and focused her camera. There was a handsome dead man with blond hair and a birthmark on his forehead. She was sure there had to be someone waiting for him. Since the Spanish married young, a woman, perhaps even a few children, who were good-looking and blond like him and who called him papa, not knowing that he was now just a slab of inert meat lying under the silvery olive trees, somewhere alongside the old road between Toledo and Madrid, in the middle of nowhere. She carefully untied the handkerchief from his neck and, with it, swatted away the flies around his face.

She didn't like focusing on things that were still; it caused her to feel apprehension. But it was better to look at the dead through the viewfinder than directly at them. It made it more bearable. While she was squatting, she could feel the grass tickling her ankles. There's nothing as solitary as a dead person, she thought, as she calculated the depth of field for the shot. And it was true. She remembered the book of Job: "Behold, this is the joy of his way; And out of the earth shall others spring." She thought of touching him, of closing his eyes. But she didn't do it.

Days later, Franco's army entered Toledo and rescued the Alcázar, clearing for the Fascists the path toward Madrid. The Republican combatants' morale plummeted to the ground.

Afterward, Gerda and Capa joined the Twelfth International Brigade, made up of German and Polish Communists from the Thälmann Battalion, whom they'd already met in Leciñena on the Aragón front. The battalion was under the command of the writer Máté Zalka, widely known as General Lukács, a very handsome Hungarian who sported a leather jacket, had a foul-mouthed and cutting sense of humor, and was also a great strategist. The brigade had to get to the Manzanares River in order to join the other regiments that were also headed to Madrid for the first major attack on the capital by Franco.

What neither of them expected to find there was Chim. Though the three of them had left Paris at the same time, the Pole had gone his own way. He was a lone hunter. He was sitting on top of a large rock, checking his equipment with the concentration of an erudite Talmudist when he saw them approaching from the other side of the road. With his index finger, he pushed his glasses up along the bridge of his nose as if to adjust his vision. He also didn't expect to see them there.

There are embraces that don't need words. A good slap on the back that can transmit all the damn words needed. A contact that's close, hard, and of rough-and-tumble men. Capa and Chim's embrace was just that. Gerda threw her arms around her friend's neck, kissing him on the forehead, on the eyes, repeating his name without end. Slightly embarrassed, he allowed himself to be loved, and joked as if all that show of emotion bothered him.

"Enough, enough, enough already . . ." he said, trying to separate himself with the shyness of a hermetic Jew. But deep down, he was happy.

It was one of those moments of extreme fulfillment that can occur sometimes in the midst of war. Two men and a woman walking along a tree-lined path, their cameras over their shoulders, twilight, a cigarette . . . At that point, each had their clocks set to their hour, their hour of death, and perhaps, in some way, the three of them knew it.

There are images that simply float through our memories, waiting for time to put them in their proper place. And though nobody can know beforehand, there's always a vague premonition, an omen, something we're not certain of, but that's there. Many years later, that would be the last image that David Seymour, Chim to his friends, would remember before he was struck down by an Egyptian sniper. It was November 10, 1956, at a border crossing, where he'd arrived with another photographer from France on an assignment to cover a prisoner exchange in the Suez Canal while peace negotiations were already underway. Dying is always a tragic event that is made more incomprehensible when it occurs during overtime, when the war has already ended. Suddenly, the rattle of machine-gun fire, and everything collapsed around him, and he found himself on the ground, vomiting blood. But before closing his eyes for good, for a split second he returned to that white point of memory: Capa, Gerda, and he, three young people walking along a trail. Smiling.

No one can choose what they remember, and Chim had no way

of knowing that chance meeting would be the last vision he'd leave behind. The Twelfth Brigade made their way through the weeds of no-man's-land. The explosions caused the trees to shake.

The only good thing about close combat was the way it caused any metaphysical anxiety to vanish before an infantry weapon. Kierkegaard and Nietzsche and Schopenhauer can all just take a hike. Philosophy was something you felt in your vitals, so that all you could think about was saving your hide, getting to a wall, reaching a crest as quickly as possible, a church, a house in ruins . . . And if the machine guns started up again, throw yourself on the ground, embed yourself within it, so you could pass under the bullets, over uneven terrain, a hole in the ground, a dugout, a mine crater, a puddle, and lap through a swamp like a buffalo up to your ears in mud, trying to advance. It was a contradictory sensation that was strangely addictive because of the incredible surge of adrenaline that's released in the act. Like removing the muscles from your body and tying them tightly along a rope. Transforming conviction into action. Awaken latent instincts. Take careful aim. A vertigo similar to what athletes must experience before a race. Reflexes. Strength. Concentration. All war correspondents have felt this sensation at least once, like Troy's warriors did, though the war Homer sung was made up of men who never would have dreamed of being characters in *The Iliad*. It's not that they had begun to like it, it was that they had never felt more alive. The Achilles syndrome. Gerda, Capa, and Chim had begun to show symptoms, though they were unable to fully understand what was happening to them. It was their first conflict.

A road full of debris, a mule ripped open and lying in a ditch; Chim went ahead to mentally prepare the photograph. Lukács talking and gesticulating a lot with his hands; Bob at his side with a camera over his shoulder, arguing, with a frown on his face. Gerda a few paces behind, smoking and laughing quietly. Click.

They shared the same attitude about danger: a kind of challenge. Something that was hard to explain that perhaps had to do

with the courage and passion of one's twenties, and its way of de-
vouring a plate of rice and a bottle of wine before heading to the
front, its desire for love in any corner, with that anger and loyalty
and those ideas. And with life. Or a certain way of living it.

They were convinced that Europe's future was at stake in Spain,
and they were fully committed to it, taking sides, abandoning any
professional distance, everyone fighting the best they could, with
the weapon that was closest to them, becoming more involved each
day. Half-reporters, half-combatants. A camera in one hand and a
pistol in the other.

Capa felt at home speaking in Hungarian with Lukács, except
for a few words here and there that he preferred to say in Spanish.
Gerda, on the other hand, didn't speak much. She liked to listen.
And she did so by paying lots of attention, her head slightly tilted,
that knowing look on her face, never missing a detail, a certain hint
of arrogance, marking the necessary distance you need when living
with men. Chim supplied the common sense, the fundamental cri-
terion of any serious and cultured Jew, though perhaps he was too
thin for that way of life and not one to flatter often, though cautious
and as trustworthy as an old seaman.

The three learned a lot from the general. How to recognize a
bullet's caliber; distinguish between an entrance and exit wound;
prepare a withdrawal before entering a high-risk area; move blindly
in the fog, like ghosts, with water up to their waists, watching the
ripples as they advance, with their hands in the air, holding up
their cameras or guns; and to fully train their ear for orientation so
that they wouldn't mistakenly head in the direction of enemy lines.
But when they finally arrived at the place where the river split, the
trenches were deserted. None of their people were waiting for them.
They were on their own.

In the distance, Madrid was a white rabbit at the mercy of
hunting hounds.

Chapter Eighteen

THE CRUCIFIED CAPITAL, declared the front-cover headlines for Capa's photo report in *Regards*. Gerda threw a thick gray wool jacket over her shoulders and sat next to Ruth on the couch of their apartment, like in the old days, just the two of them. On the other side of the window, the day was overcast, with that touch of fog that can sometimes cover Paris's rooftops with sadness. Her friend was the mother rock to all those who returned late or early from battle. Capa, Chim, her . . . Ruth Cerf listened to them all with that generous attitude that only truly maternal people can have. Attentive eyes, an understanding forehead, with that protective instinct that women used to have when they buttoned up a coat properly and wrapped their children's scarves around them on chilly mornings. Sitting on top of the Moroccan table, next to two cups of tea and a small plate of Breton cookies, the magazine was open to an image of aerial bombing. Gerda looked at the faces of women from the working-class neighborhood of Vallecas, captured only minutes after they had returned home to find their houses in flames and their neighbors buried beneath the rubble. A sloping street with skeletal trees and two militiamen sharing the same rifle, waiting for the opportune moment to shoot at the enemy. A young refugee mother with three small children on a platform in the metro station. Gray countryside and burning stables on the other side of the highway. Several brigadists with backpacks walking in a straight line with their heads down, one step in front of the other, staring at the footprints they were leaving behind in the mud, concentrated, like warriors before combat. A close-up of a militiawoman, nearly an adolescent, squatting, aiming her Mauser from a barricade in front of the School of Medicine. Gerda passed from one scene to another and her mind always returned to Madrid, to that well of memories that she couldn't stop submerging herself in since she'd returned. After all the intensity she had experienced in Spain, she couldn't bear the routine of Parisian life.

She took a sip of tea and the longing embraced her lips. She missed it. She remembered the Gran Vía during the last days of September, just before her return trip, and how it rained artillery shells day and night. Or how floodlights pierced the sky and the building's facades on a revolving angle. The rooftops of Madrid de los Austrias; the Telefónica building that housed the government press office from where she had sent dispatches several times, hunched over, while the projectiles passed over her head. The Calle de Alcalá; the tall windows of the Círculo de Bellas Artes. Those blue intersections and geometrical formations on the ceiling of her hotel room where her mind had now wandered.

"We have to go down to the shelter," she had said when it seemed the buzzing of the engines was only escalating, followed by the crisp and tight rattle of antiaircraft fire the day the Fascists launched their second deadly attack on the city.

They were in the Hotel Florida. They had just returned from Casa del Campo, in the western part of the city where the Republicans had entrenched themselves and built barricades with cushions, doors, and even suitcases they'd taken from the Northern Station's lockers. They'd been able to get some great shots. Capa would review the images, looking at them up against the lamplight, his eye pressed up against the magnifying loupe, marking the best negatives with a cross. As she watched him work, from the foot of the door, Gerda felt an uncontrollable tenderness toward him. He was both a child playing with his favorite toy and a grown man completely dedicated to a job that was challenging, mysterious, essential, and for which he sometimes risked his life.

When he turned around, she surprised him with a kiss. And he just stood there for a few seconds with his arms open, more from shock than indecision, before unbuckling his belt and pushing her softly onto the bed so she could feel his hardness over her lower abdomen. She opened her legs, holding him prisoner inside, while she kissed his neck and the rough stubble on his face that tasted like sweat—masculine and pungent.

"We should head down," she said in a mumbled voice lacking conviction, while the sirens wailed outside, and he entered deeper. Firm, serious, without ever taking his eyes off her, as if he wanted to store her forever in the camera obscura of his memory, just as she was in that moment, with her gathered eyebrow, her hungering mouth, half-open, moving her head slightly from side to side, as she always did when she was about to come. That's when he held on tightly to her hips and entered her even further, slowly, deep down inside her, to release himself long and languidly, until letting out a groan and dropping his head onto her shoulder. The blue floodlights swirling across the ceiling. She had taught him to declare himself like that, noisily. She enjoyed hearing him express his pleasure in that animal-like manner. Though for reasons having to do with intimacy, modesty, and male shyness, he was hesitant to do it. He had never shouted during an orgasm as he did that day, with the deafening sounds of planes passing right over their heads and a series of air-defense explosions across the street. They remained in bed silent for a while in the midst of those bluish shadows circling the ceiling, while Gerda caressed his back, and Madrid breathed through its wounds, and he looked at her in silence, as if from a distant shore, with those eyes of a handsome Gypsy.

She placed her teacup back into the tray with the same dreamy expression on her face.

"I'm going back to Spain," she told Ruth.

Capa had been in Madrid since November. Thanks to the success of his work, especially "The Falling Soldier," he'd been offered a new assignment. All the French editors had already discovered a while back that the famous Robert Capa was none other than the Hungarian André Friedmann. But his photographs had greatly improved, and he went to such great lengths to risk getting them that they went along with his game. They felt obliged to pay him his going rate. His *nom de guerre* had completely devoured that ragged, if slightly naive man raised in a working-class neighborhood in Pest. Now he was Capa, Robert, Bobby, Bob . . . He no longer needed a costume; the world of journalism had accepted him as he was, and he'd done his part to take on the role, firmly believing in his character, remaining loyal to him until the very end. More than ever, he believed in himself and in his work. With hopes his photographs could help gain intervention from the Western powers in backing the Republican government, he had given up on that alleged journalistic impartiality, up to his nose in a war that would only wind up shattering his life.

In his letters, he'd tell Gerda how the *Madrileños* would risk themselves in front of the tanks, attacking them with dynamite and bottles filled with gasoline that they ignited with the tips of their cigarettes because matches were scarce. When modern German machine guns opened fire, they'd retaliate with their old Mauser rifles. David versus Goliath. The fall of the city seemed inevitable. Madrid, however, resisted the beatings with a courage that earned it mythical levels of coverage in publications such as *Regards, Vu, Zürcher Illustrierte, Life, Weekly Illustrated*, along with all the major newspapers of the world, whose print runs approached the 100,000 mark. The Spanish Civil War had become the first conflict to be photographed and transmitted on a daily basis. "A cause without images is not only a forgotten cause. It's also a lost cause," he wrote in a letter to Gerda, dated November 18, the same day that Hitler and Mussolini officially recognized Franco as the Spanish head of state.

She was proud of him, of course she was. The Robert Capa invention had also been her idea in the first place. But the fact that several of the best photographs she'd taken in Spain were published without her name, and credited to his, caused her a certain unease. Perhaps she'd been mistaken, or maybe the moment had come to rethink their professional relationship and convert it into one with more equal footing. The brand "Capa & Taro" sounded pretty good.

But war was the territory of men. Women didn't count.

"I'm nobody, I'm nobody"—she remembered how he had once said this at the edge of the Seine, when his first report on Sarre didn't appear with his name on it. It felt as though a thousand years had passed since then, and now it was she who felt neglected. She didn't exist. Sometimes she'd look in the bathroom mirror and carefully observe each new wrinkle in bewilderment, as if she feared that time, life, or her own will would wind up destroying what was left of her dreams. A woman in a blind spot.

"Are you all right?" he had asked several hours after that air-raid siren had sounded in their room at the Hotel Florida, and the dim, striped light of daybreak entered. She had shot up violently. Having awakened sweating, her hair soaked, her forehead clammy, and her heart galloping in her chest like a runaway horse.

"I had a nightmare," she managed to say, when her breathing was finally back to normal.

"Fuck, Gerda, you look like you just went to hell and back." It was as if she had suddenly aged ten years, her thin face, the violet-colored circles under her eyes, her worn expression. "Would you like a glass of water?"

"Yes."

She didn't know where in hell she'd gone, but from that point on, she found herself feeling profoundly, darkly uncertain. And it was hard for her to recover. Capa brought her the glass, but she wasn't able to hold it. Her hands were shaking, as if out of nowhere she'd lost love's protective shield. He brought the water up to her lips for her to drink, but a good portion of it ran down her chin, wetting her shirt and the top fold of the sheet. If everything she had learned would not remain inscribed somewhere, what would have been the purpose of her life? She rested her head on the pillow again but was unable to fall back asleep, watching how the morning light began to filter itself little by little over the ceiling of their room, thinking that death was probably a lot like the blackness from her nightmare. A nearby border to nonexistence.

His letters from the front plunged her into a contradictory state. A part of her feared for his life while the other deeply envied the sensations he described and that she knew very well: to have your back up against the slope of ditch swearing in Aramaic at those Fascist sons-of-bitches and the mothers that gave birth to them. That bone-chilling silence after the fire of the howitzers, a silence like no other, that smell of the earth's proximity, that physical certainty that only the now matters, and afterward, less than two hundred yards from the front line, the bars on the Gran Vía with their delicious coffee with cream, served in a tall, tubular glass. Confectionery after the battle. He had already been poisoned by the war's virus and he didn't know it.

She couldn't stop humming the songs she'd learned in Spain.

Madrid you're so resistant,
Madrid you're so resistant
Madrid you're so resistant . . .
Little mama, the bombings
the bombings . . .

She sang them in the shower, as she cooked, while she looked out the window, and Paris felt too small for her, because the only world that mattered began on the other side of the Pyrenees. At last, she had found a terra firma that would not sink under her feet. Others called themselves Spaniards for a lot less than that.

Ruth knew her well. She knew that Gerda was not one to wait patiently, like Penelope, for her man to return, weaving and unweaving the tapestry of memory. With resignation, Ruth listened to her, like a mother or an older sister, her eyebrows raised, a wave of hair clipped up and hanging over one side of her forehead, her bathrobe sealed over her chest, interrupting only when necessary to offer a piece of advice already predestined to fall upon deaf ears. She watched Gerda smoke with that smile apparently devoid of intentions, and knew that she had already come to a decision.

Whether Alliance Photo offered her a contract or not, with credentials or without them, she was going to Spain.

She had always been like this. Take the first train, make a quick decision. It's here or there. It's black or white. Choose.

"No, Ruth," she said in an attempt to defend herself from the comment her friend had made aloud. "The reality is I've never been able to choose. I didn't choose what happened in Leipzig, I didn't choose to come to Paris, I didn't choose to abandon my family, my brothers, I didn't choose to fall in love. Nor did I even choose to become a photographer. I chose nothing. Whatever came my way, I dealt with it as I could." She got up and began playing with an amber bead, tossing it between her hands. "My script was written by others. And I have this sense of always having lived in someone else's shadow, first Georg, then Bob . . . It's time for me to take the reins of my own life. I don't want to be anyone's property. Maybe I'm not as good a photographer as he is, but I have my own way of doing things, and when I focus, and calculate the distance, and press the shutter release, I know it's my vision that I'm defending, and no one in the world—not he, not Chim, not Fred Stein, not Henri, no one—could ever photograph what I see, since it comes naturally to me."

"It sounds like you're a little upset with him," said Ruth.

Feeling uncomfortable, Gerda sank her hands into the pockets of her slacks and hunched her shoulders. It was true she felt betrayed when her name didn't appear credited for the photos. Capa's success had relegated her to the background. But it wasn't easy for her to express the sensation that had taken hold of her in the last few weeks. The deeper her love, the bigger the gap she placed between them. She began to need a certain distance and felt that he should allow her the space she considered appropriate. Professional independence was the key to loving herself. How does one love and at the same time fight against that which one loves?

"I'm not upset," she said. "Just a bit tired."

Even though she rejected her religious beliefs, she couldn't stop herself from being Jewish. Her vision of the world included a tangible line dating back to her ancestors. She had been raised on the stories from the Old Testament. Abraham, Isaac, Sarah, Jacob . . . The same way she loved family tradition she would have detested dying without a name.

Chapter Nineteen

Never had she seen cafés so packed. Not even in Paris. It was normal to have to stand and wait until a seat was freed. Since the Republicans had moved to Valencia, many correspondents had been evacuated to the coastal city now populated by civilians who'd fled the bombings in Madrid. The highway to Puerto de Contreras was being guarded by men from the Rosal column. Dark-eyed, a country folk's gait, sideburns, lively-colored capes, and a pistol on their hip; they were the real kind of anarchists. Spaniards from a fierce caste who helped their women with the children, carried them in pairs over their backs, but when it came to men who'd abandoned their barricades, they had no pity. Eyeing them furiously, with a bull's disdain toward the tame lamb. Sheer brilliance. There was no excusing them for abandoning the capital to its own fate. Many were obliged to go back. But when sick and hungry children arrived by night from far away, the lights from the city high above, with their sacks over their shoulders, they showed themselves, smiling.

"Cheer up, my friends," they'd say. "Here you'll surely get sick of eating so much rice."

Valencia, full of bright lights and a view of the sea. A dream.

Gerda had just arrived. She looked all around without being able to find one empty table. The Ideal Room café, with its large windows that opened onto Calle de la Paz, was the war correspondents' favorite. The place was always packed with journalists, diplomats, writers, spies, and brigadists from all four cardinal points, milling around underneath its ceiling fans, with their leather jackets, "blond cigarettes," and their international songs.

The sight of a woman entering alone caused a stir at the tables. Her beret tightly in place and a revolver on her hip.

"Gerda, what on earth are you doing here?" She heard the voice of a tall German man who had stood up to greet her from the other end of the café.

It was Alfred Kantorowicz, an old friend from Paris. They had spent many hours together at the Capoulade's gatherings. He was attractive and wore the round glasses of an intellectual. With the help of Walter Benjamin and Gustav Regler, he had been able to establish the Association of German Writers in Exile. Along with Chim, Ruth, and Capa, Gerda had attended many of their events, which included poetry readings and short plays. Today, Kantorowicz was the political commissary for the Thirteenth Brigade.

She took a seat next to him at the table and introduced herself to the other brigadists as a special correspondent for *Ce Soir*.

"It's a new publication," she added humbly.

The magazine hadn't yet released its first edition on newsstands, but they had all heard talk about it, since it was well known in the Communist Party's circles and because it was run by Louis Aragon.

The café's cosmopolitan atmosphere could be detected in the smoke: Gauloises Bleues, Gitanes, Ideales, Valencian stogies, Pall-Mall, and even Camel and Lucky Strike. That tribe could resemble a map with all the tributaries of a faraway river. French, German, Hungarian, English, American . . . So that borders were no longer important. Once in Spain, they removed their country's clothes in order to change into the blue uniform or olive-green fatigues. Erase nations. That was the war's lesson. For them, Spain was the symbol of all countries, a representation of the very notion of a universe ridiculed. There were metalworkers, doctors, students, typesetters, poets, scientists such as the biologist J.B.S. Haldane, deliberate and self-righteous, sporting an aviator jacket he bought at a store in Piccadilly Circus. Gerda felt right at home. Out of all the cigarettes being offered to her, she chose a Gauloises Bleues, and let the smoke pass through her lungs, the way all the words and sensations passed through her body.

"And Capa?" the German asked, puzzled, after a while. He was used to always seeing them together.

Gerda shrugged. A long silence. Kantorowicz couldn't take his eyes off the warm triangle of her neckline.

"I'm not his babysitter," she said proudly.

Valencia was courteous, generous, and aromatic. In those days, it was the war's most amiable face. They were all passing through on the way to somewhere, and they rushed through the waiting as best they could. First thing in the morning, they'd cross the Plaza de Castelar, with its large circular openings to light and ventilate the underground flower market, toward Hotel Victoria, where the Republican government was staying, to see if there was any news. The correspondents usually ate at the restaurant in Hotel Londres, especially on Thursdays, when they served paella. The maître d', dressed in a tux, would approach the tables remorsefully and say:

"Please excuse the service and the food . . . Since the Committee's arrival, this is no longer what it used to be."

Valencia's people were kind lovers of life, slightly loud, and always telling sexually explicit jokes. Gerda, who was now more or less able to get by in the language, still found it hard to understand what they were saying. But she soon learned how to incorporate the Valencian *che* into her vocabulary, and people immediately wanted to adopt her. There are people who, without even trying, are automatically loved. It's something you're born with, like the way you laugh as you tell a joke in a low voice. Gerda was one of those people. Languages came easily to her. She could interpret each accent with the fluency of a musician improvising a new melody. Pronounce swear words with such elegant grace that she could seduce anyone. She listened with her head slightly tilted to the side, a complicit air about her, like a mischievous child. Within the feminine canon, she wasn't especially pretty, but the war had given her a different kind of beauty; that of a survivor. Much too thin and angular, with eyebrows that were arched and ironic, always dressed in a blue uniform or a military shirt, and with a charm that tempted everyone. For her suitors, Capa's absence signified an open season, and she began to enjoy the pleasures of being courted. The waiters reserving the best tables for her. The silent rivalry among the men around her, who competed to buy her drinks, offer her the latest news, make her laugh, or take her dancing to one of the salons on Calle del Trinquete de Caballeros.

DANCING IS THE ANTEROOM TO THE BROTHEL: LET'S SHUT IT DOWN, read a black-and-red poster on the door, endorsed by the acronym FAI.

"The owner can't be an anarchist," said Gerda after someone translated it for her.

"Of course he is. And a hard-core anarchist. He is one of the founders of the Federación Anarquista Ibérica."

"So how does he manage to keep this place open then?"

"Well, since prohibition is an act of government, it's his way of showing that no one gives him orders. You know: No Gods, No Masters."

Anarchists! So independent, so loyal, so humane. Spanish to the core. Gerda smiled on the inside.

Other times, a group would go down to Malvarrosa beach to eat shrimp and watch the boats. That's what she liked most. Sitting in the sand and watching the Grao fishermen use oxen to pull the sailboats to shore.

First, they'd make them go into the water until they were up to their knees, then they'd yoke the oxen and strap on the boats' cables, and they'd tow them to the sand. Several pairs of oxen dragging a small sailboat out of the sea, with a line of shining waves that would break onto the sand. She'd stay there alone for hours, smoking and looking out into the distance, while the salty air refreshed her skin and her memories.

Not all of it was free time. She had to complete her assignments. Now she was a self-employed photojournalist. All her images were signed "Photo Taro." She had never felt so in charge of her own life. She crouched below a cloister's arch in the Instituto Luis Vives, her knees together, her pupils contracted to pinpoints. Right in front of her, a column lined up in a Popular Army formation. She set the foreground in focus, a vanishing point perspective. Click. As a contrast to photographs of war, she also liked to shoot images of everyday life: a couple in Santa Catalina drinking *horchata* in the afternoon, a band contest beneath a diptych with the portraits of Machado and García Lorca, young boys taking lessons in the bullring. Valencia had found a place in her heart. The city was open, sensual, and hospitable. For all the refugees that had arrived hungry from the fronts, that place was like a paradise of abundance, the promised land, with Barrachina's shop window always filled with groceries and supplies. But every day, the front was getting closer, and from Plaza de Castelar's balconies, one began to see other things: the arrival of crowds from Malaga fleeing the massive shootings. People in espadrilles, with raw feet and faces broken from fear.

She didn't think twice about it. Her credentials were valid only in Valencia, so she went with her camera gear slung over her shoulder to the propaganda office, within the Municipality of Defense, to obtain permission to cover the exodus of the thousands of refugees arriving from Andalusia's eastern coast. It wasn't easy to get a pass. In order to turn down those who wanted to take advantage of the situation, the authorities were studying each petition with a magnifying glass. In certain European bohemian circles, the idea of taking a kind of "war tour" had become fashionable. They were people looking for thrills, trying to free themselves from the boredom of their pedestrian lives by checking into the best hotels in Valencia or Barcelona at the expense of the press office, as if they were there to see the bulls, standing behind the barricade, watching from the sidelines how the Spanish were killing one another. The Republican authorities would not stand for it. So, a majority of the correspondents had to wait for authorization and a space in a car while they rolled their cigarettes and compulsively typed up reports and telephoned, in foreign languages, claims that were never received.

However, Gerda was given her safe-conduct in less than ten minutes, in addition to having her pass validated, with the Alliance of Antifascist Intellectuals' stamp on it. She knew how to get by on her own: having a way with people, the ability to be understood in five languages, a killer smile, and a bureaucracy-proof obstinacy.

For days she watched refugees moving along the coastal highway. First, the mule-drawn carts, then the women and the elderly carrying bundles on their backs, followed by frightened children with dirty faces, then the rest. Desperate, barefooted, exhausted, with that faraway look in their eyes that people get when it no longer matters if they continue forward or head back. One hundred fifty thousand people who had abandoned their homes and their entire lives, running away from the terror toward Almería, and later to Valencia, searching for the closest Republican shelter without knowing that the worst was yet to come. Hell. Franco's tanks following them overland and brutally mowing them down. Italian and German planes bombing them from above and gunboats intensifying their attack along the coast. It was a mousetrap. Cliffs on one side, a wall of rock on the other. There was no escape. Mothers blindfolding their children so they wouldn't see the bodies in the ditches. One hundred twenty-five miles on foot without anything to eat. Every once in a while, one would hear the purr of motors and overloaded militia trucks would arrive with faded green canvases, covered in dust, falling apart, and devastated. Parents begging them on their knees to take their children, knowing that if the militia accepted, they'd probably never see their children again. The worst episode of the war. The majority of the refugees were in a state of shock. Others collapsed from exhaustion while the planes started up their next attack, weaving their intricate spiderwebs in the air. No one ran for cover. It didn't matter anymore.

Gerda didn't know where to look. To her, it was the end of the world. She saw a very tall woman transporting a flour sack on the back of a white horse, and like an automaton, she pressed the shutter button. She believed she could be delirious. No one buried the dead and there wasn't enough strength to salvage the wounded.

At nightfall, she heard a strange murmur. Vibrations, rustling, banging, a set of headlights straightening themselves out in the darkness and coming around a curve. She walked toward the lights as if there was no longer a world left around her. It was a hospital's mobile medical unit. A man dressed in a white robe stained with blood, like a butcher's apron, was wrapping a bandage around an old man's head. Norman Bethune, the Canadian doctor, looked as though he'd been brought back to life. Gaunt, bearded, bloodshot eyes. He had just returned from three long days of performing blood transfusions and picking up children along the way.

That sadness could be a feeling so close to hate was something Gerda had never realized until then. First, she lifted the oil lamp's wick to expand the light's diameter around her. Then she threw a blanket over her shoulders and walked in the direction of the ambulance. She could hear the complaints of the sick, the voice of a mother speaking softly to her child. In the back of the truck, there was a board that was used as an operating table. At any moment after sundown, if a vein is sliced in the darkness, the blood turns black as petroleum. The worst part was the smell. At that moment, she would have done anything to be with Capa. He'd know exactly what to say to calm her. He had a gift for making people smile during the worst moments.

She remained absorbed in her thoughts, finishing a cigarette, remembering the touch of his rough and confident hands, those loyal spaniel eyes, his way of breathing on her neck after lovemaking, his self-deprecating humor capable of also saying something presumptuous to make her furious and fixing it again with that look that erased everything. Gentle, witty, egotistical. Damn that Hungarian, she thought to herself again, almost saying it out loud so she could stifle the sob rising to her mouth. Pale, she walked alongside the ditches, among the piles of dead bodies, with a lost expression on her face.

Just as she thought she was going to die if she didn't see a familiar face soon, she heard a snap, like when a candle extinguishes itself. Someone had just used their nail to break open a vial of morphine. Before he turned around, she had already recognized him from the back. His long legs, the rolled-up sleeves on his arms, currently digging inside a first-aid kit, an air of Gary Cooper.

"Ted."

He turned around to look at her. They hadn't seen each other since Cerro Muriano. Her nineteen-year-old guardian angel had aged. She walked over to him slowly, placing her forehead against his chest, and for the first time since she'd been in Spain, she let herself cry without worrying who might see her. Silently, without saying a word, unable to hold back the tears, while Ted Allan stroked her head gently, as confused and quiet as she was. His right hand between her blond hair and the fabric of his shirt. That physical contact was the only possible consolation in the midst of the river of bodies. If felt as though the tears were coming not from her chest but from her throat, and blocking her breathing. She remained like this a good while, crying her heart out, after seven months of war trying hard not to fall apart.

Hell.

Chapter Twenty

I'm twenty-five years old and I know this war is the end of a part of my life. The end, perhaps, of my youth. Sometimes it seems it's going to do away with the entire world's youth. Spain's war has done something to all of us. We're no longer the same. This era we're living in is so full of change that it's difficult to recognize who we were just two years ago. I can't even imagine what's ahead . . ." She was wrapped up in a blanket, with her red notebook resting on her knees and the last bit of light disappearing into the horizon. It was her favorite time of day. If she had been a writer, she would have chosen the twilight to begin working on her novels, as her special time to allow the mind to wander. No lover could ever cross over into that exclusive territory. From those heights and along the sloping rooftops, she could see areas that had been hit by the bombs, the acres of farmland destroyed. Contemplating the tormented place she now found herself in—within Spain—she placed her pen on the paper's white surface and continued writing. "Over the last few months I traveled through this country soaking up all it has to offer. I've seen a sacrificed and broken people, women who remain strong, men with strange and tragic visions, and men with a sense of humor. This country is so mysterious, so theirs, so ours. I've seen it soften and crumble during an attack and rise again the next day with freshly formed scars. I still haven't grown completely tired of seeing it, but I will one day. That I know."

The field hospital occupied a section of the esplanade that was tucked away in the darkness so that it wouldn't attract the attention of enemy planes. Many of the refugees slept beneath the trucks' canvases, wrapped in blankets. Children whose feet were wrapped in bandages huddled together on top of the piles of sandbags. Starting from Almería, the government attempted to evacuate everyone who was in condition to travel via bus, train, or boat, but the situation had become overwhelming.

Capa arrived on February 14, when the worst had already passed. He'd flown in on a small plane from Toulouse to Valencia. Several of his colleagues had remained in the city, awaiting permission. With rows of tables packed with typewriters and untidy mountains of dirty carbon paper, the Press Office could not keep up with all the requests. Seeing how difficult it was to find another form of transportation, he decided to hire his own taxi and take the Sollana highway smack up against rice fields, and continue alongside the River Júcar to Andalusia. He wasn't aware how much the war was rousing his emotions. Aside from the driver, he was all alone with his character, prepared to remain loyal to him under all circumstances, in a kind of limbo where life becomes the legend of what you make of it. His Leica on his arm, his eyes glued to the odometer. When he arrived, he saw Gerda standing against the light, extending a sheet over a clearing in the grass while Ted Allan prepared bandage strips with calamine on a tray.

"I didn't know you had become a nurse," he said with a touch of sarcasm to his tone. Half-smiling, somewhere between smooth and wary. He was mad at her, though he didn't have a concrete reason to be, and that upset him even more.

"You're too late," she said, subtly crossing swords with him, not specifying whether she was referring to covering the refugees' exodus or for the rest of her life.

Capa couldn't handle it when she entrenched herself behind a wall of pride with her doublespeak. In her fatigues and with that pale face and the imperiousness of a medieval warrior, her beauty radiated with unbearable intensity for him. He looked at her, waiting for her to say something more. But there wasn't anything else to say. For now.

The ice began to melt as the days went by, despite the chilling frankness of the Canadian camaraderie of Ted and Norman. When projectile missiles began falling over the city, they decided to move with the trucks and their tents to an old farmhouse. The building was nearly in ruins. There were steps missing in the stairwell, and the banisters had become dismantled. Some of the rooms in the east wing had no roofs, which made it feel as if they were in an aviary. When you opened a door, there was the landscape, but the kitchen had remained intact. That's where Dr. Bethune prepared his mixtures of sodium citrate in order to conserve the blood he used for transfusions. Capa liked to joke around with the children, creating shadow-plays on the walls, moving his fingers with a white handkerchief. Gerda watched him as he clowned around, and smiled.

The second night, she removed her boots and entered his tent crouched on all fours. When, without further ado, she felt his hand caressing her skin, she knew that what was about to happen was exactly what she had wished for. The masculine taste of his lips, his mouth whispering words that were both sweet and obscene, down below, between her legs, moving slowly, confidently, prolonging each caress to its limit, driving her mad until she'd surrender all her principles. At the last minute she looked up toward the roof of the tent, searching for a place to grab on to but not finding a single handle. She felt more vulnerable than ever. Be free, defend your independence, belong to no one, fall in love so that you can't bear it. Everything was so complicated.

Gerda had already heard it from that Camila woman, a mind-blower of a Gypsy fortune-teller, who was part-deaf, straight-backed, and had arrived from Cádiz.

"*Niña*, loving a man is more work than blowing up a train."

The woman knew what she was talking about. She had blown up a few of her own. She was in her fifties, sporting a black skirt and long, dark, straight hair that was parted in the middle and held up in the back with a gold comb. A woman as hardy as a mule and with hands like granite. She would tie her little ones with cords to her waist, and when they reached the point of exhaustion and started to complain, saying they couldn't go on walking, she'd whip them with the ends of the cords, like goats, forcing them to keep going. Afterward, when she noticed that they really couldn't go on, she'd carry them in pairs up the side of the mountain, climbing up and down to fetch them as many times as was necessary. Capa would always tease her when he saw her drinking from a wineskin like a road worker. They got along well despite her thick Andalusian accent and her being hard of hearing. The Gypsy soul.

Feeling playful, Gerda extended her hand out in front of her. The woman opened it, passing her thumb carefully over her palm. She held it in her hands for a while, then shut it without saying a word. They sat drinking coffee beside a campfire. Gerda and Capa had planned to leave very early the next morning and wanted to say good-bye. They'd decided to continue to the bridge in Arganda where violent combat had recently broken out.

"So what did you see, Camila?" asked Capa, with a cigarette hanging out of his mouth.

"Your girl's a reasonable one, Hungarian, but watch out for her bites." Capa's neck still showed signs of their recent love tussle, an eggplant-colored hickey just below his left ear.

"She should have been a vampire," he joked, flapping his arms like a bat in flight, "a vampiress, probably the most dangerous of their kind. *Tadarida Teniotis.*"

"She'll be a good wife if you can get her to stay on course."

"*Por los cojones!*" said Gerda in perfect Spanish.

They laughed at her comeback. It was amusing to them to hear a charming foreigner swear like a mule-driver but with such elegance. She could strip away the original meaning of any rude interjection and provoke you with it. It was like watching an Angora cat hunt down a mouse with the street smarts of a stray.

"And what do you see in her future?" asked Ted, who had already experienced just how precise the Gypsy's fortunes could be. He was sitting next to Gerda with his knees bent and his head propped on top. Though being in Gerda's presence sometimes caused him to blush, he adored Capa like an older brother. Not so long ago, in Paris, on a gloomy, cloudy day, the two of them, very drunk, comforted one another with alcohol and conversation, while one of the harshest sunrises of their lives awaited them. The Canadian was frank and loyal. He would have preferred to kill himself rather than betray either of them. Deep down, the war was tearing at the delicate weaving of his affections. His question was of value, a guardian angel's question based on the many things that perhaps he'd foreseen or intuited were about to happen. "You're not going to offer us anything?"

"Nothing."

"Please say whatever you wish," said Gerda, attempting to encourage her while showing her respect. "I don't believe in these things."

"So what do you believe in, girl?"

"In my ideas."

"Ideas, ideas . . ." *that* Camila woman repeated to herself as if she were praying.

"You've left us intrigued," protested Capa, winking at the Gypsy. He was sure she was trying to withhold a certain disillusion of the heart.

"Go on," insisted Gerda, "tell me what you saw from reading my palm. I'd like to know."

"Nothing." This time her tone was sharp and her face serious; shaking her head as she was getting up to leave. "I saw nothing, little one."

They left at the dawn of a cloudy day, surrounded by white-washed puddles, a sky of indecisive tones that said its good-byes with the sadness of a hotel room, still blurry from last night's ciga-rettes and to which one knows they'll never return.

The trip might have been peaceful if it wasn't for the potholes and the constant bumps to the head. Along their entire journey west, they came upon several rows of military trucks carrying old Packards, combat cars, and cargo under worn-out canvases. The highway grew more chaotic as they approached the front of Jarama. On both sides of the gravel path, you could see columns of smoke floating between the earth and the sky. The rebels had attempted to block the Madrid-Valencia highway and leave the capital with-out its main supply route. But the Republicans fought tooth and nail along the Arganda Bridge and were able to salvage the road-way. By nightfall, Gerda and Capa had arrived at the International Brigades' headquarters in Morata de Tajuña, a plain that was sur-rounded by wheat fields that would soon be reaped by shrapnel. But at that hour, the camp was quiet.

There are voices that can rustle the trees in the same way a rifle can when it's fired. On the night they arrived, the voice Gerda and Capa heard was precisely one of those.

Ol' Man River
That Ol' Man River . . .

More than two hundred people were sitting in a large circle with their legs crossed Indian-style. Practically ceremonial.

"Shit, it's the black man . . ." exclaimed Capa, completely moved by whom he saw. It was Paul Robeson, a six-foot-three son of an es-caped slave from New Jersey, with a football player's broad, sloping chest that allowed his grand voice to resonate like a pipe organ. He was standing in the middle of that plain surrounded by an audience of shadows that broke out into a standing ovation when the grandson of slaves concluded with a last deep note that elevated itself over all borders.

Hundreds of faces that remained still and tense, overcome with emotion, holding their breaths, listening to the spiritual black man who seemed as if he'd been plucked right out of the cotton fields along the Mississippi. Gerda could feel that music, not hitting her over the head the way the Psalms could, but in her gut. There was something profoundly Biblical in that solitary music. The darkness, the smell of the fields, the gathering of people from so many places. All of them so young, practically kids, like Pati Edney, an eighteen-year-old British woman who fell in love riding on an ambulance's running board on the front at Aragón. Or John Cornford, a twenty-year-old Englishman with a leather jacket and a boyish smile, who smoked one filterless cigarette after another, and who would have been an excellent poet if a bullet hadn't exploded in his lungs in the mountains of Córdoba. Gerda and Capa had met up with some of them in Leciñena or in Madrid, when the Fascists arrived at the edge of the Manzanares and they joined General Lukacs's brigade. Gerda could still see the writer Gustav Regler's face as he was being carried out of the rubble on a stretcher by two militiamen after an attack. He was a very tall German fellow whom Capa had gotten drunk with during the time of the battles in Casa de Campo, and who had confessed he'd fallen head over heels in love with a married woman much older than he. The American Ben Leider, in his aviator glasses, posing with his entire squadron in front of the Policarpov I-15 in which he had defended Madrid until the aircraft was eventually shot down. Every time a biplane fighter took off on a mission, they'd pass over his grave in Colmenar de Oreja cemetery and say hello from the air. Frida Knight, who fed the pigeons bread crumbs in the Plaza Santa Ana and would become furious when Fascists' howitzers blew them away. Ludwig Renn, his left arm covered in pink scars from machine-gun wounds. Through the lenses of her round spectacles, the cruelty of the fight and the disconcerted look in Simone Weil's eyes. Charles Donnelly, with a carpenter's pencil tucked behind his ear, who liked writing poems by candlelight in the plains of Morata. Alex McDade, clever and blunt, who could make everyone laugh with his typically Scottish humor, sitting on the sidewalk eating tuna from a can while Franco's planes bombed every inch of the Gran Vía. Americans from the Lincoln Brigade, Bulgarians and Yugoslavians from the Dimitrov Battalion, Poles from the Dombrowski Battalion, Germans from the Thälmann Brigade and from the Edgar André Battalion, French from the Marseillaise Battalion, Cubans, Russians . . . Gerda thought she might run into Georg somewhere. She knew from his last letter that he'd spent the past three months fighting in Spain, but chance did not choose to lower the bridge for them to meet.

"I love black music," said Gerda.

Paul Robeson's singing had enlivened the group with such a charge of emotion that they raised their fists to their temples and shouted: "Cheers! Cheers! . . ."

Afterward, they walked toward their tents, the plain becoming more visible as their eyes grew accustomed to the dark, a breeze from the wheat fields causing the tents to undulate slightly, a night that was cold and flat, that could purify all sounds and smells. And as if it had been covered by a bell jar, the murmur of the camp suddenly faded away. Holding hands, a special kind of harmony between them, almost geological, nocturnal. Capa found those lands beautiful enough to die there.

"If I offered you my life, you would reject it, right?" It was neither a complaint nor a reproach.

She didn't answer.

Capa had never loved anyone as much, and it made him think about his own mortality. The more she demanded her independence, the more unattainable she appeared, and the more his need to have her grew. For the first time in his life, he felt possessive.

He hated her self-sufficiency, or when she chose to sleep alone. It was impossible to get her out of his head; he was thinking obsessively about every centimeter of her skin, her voice, the things she'd say when she argued over the slightest matter, the way she crawled into his tent and pressed up against his body, pouting softly like a saint or an Andalusian virgin.

Turning toward her, in order to touch her wrist gently, he said: "Marry me."

Gerda did a double take when she heard his words. It wasn't confusion. Just that she was a bit moved. Months ago, she would have happily accepted.

Facing him, she looked directly and gently into his eyes, holding back the consolation of a caress, as if she doubted him or owed him an explanation. She felt the powerlessness of all that she could not say, searching for any word that could save her. She remembered an old Polish proverb: "If you clip a lark's wings, it will be yours. But then it couldn't fly. And what you love about it is its flight." She preferred not to say anything. Lowering her eyes so that her pity wouldn't humiliate him more, she let go of him and continued to walk toward the tent, aware of the powerful density of the earth below her feet, with a deep shame inside tearing at her soul, thinking about how difficult it would be to love someone else as much as she loved that Hungarian who had looked at her with resignation, as if he could read her thoughts, a smile with hints of sadness and irony to it, knowing that it was the pact they had made. Here, there, nowhere . . .

Chapter Twenty-one

The old manor was still holding up after months of occupation. It was located on 7 Calle del Marqués del Duero and had been expropriated from the Marqués Heredia Spínola's heirs in order to be converted into the Alliance of Anti-Fascist Intellectuals' main office. The building creaked at all of its seams; it was ugly, overly stately, decorated with funereal furniture and thick velvet curtains, but it harbored an entire hidden city within. The Alliance's salons were constantly overflowing with actors, journalists, artists, writers, both foreign and Spanish, and, most important, poets, such as Rafael Alberti, who served as its secretary. In the months between winter and spring that year, several figures passed through: Pablo Neruda, who still remained Chile's consul in Madrid; César Vallejo, a Peruvian open-form poet; Luis Cernuda, always elegant with his freshly groomed hair and trimmed beard; León Felipe, who kept count of the number of dead from aerial bombings; Miguel Hernández, the pastor poet from Orihuela, his face blackened by the sun upon returning from the front with his shaved head and peasant's gait, barely lifting his feet off the ground.

In the dim light of the hallways, Gerda passed eighteenth-century murals on the walls in silence. When she arrived at her room on the second floor, she opened the door to a walnut wardrobe and discovered a collection of period pieces, just hanging there on the rod, which had belonged to several generations of Spanish nobles: austere frock coats, lace gowns, admiral uniforms with blue fabric and gold buttons, muslin dresses that smelled of camphor.

"It's fantastic!" she said to Capa, her eyes big, like a little girl's.

Around four or five of them all had the same idea. They removed those dusty relics from the wardrobe and slid them down the polished mahogany banister, releasing a flurry of moths. Shortly after, the main hall of mirrors had become an improvised theater, with everyone in their costumes interpreting the part they'd been given to play. Capa was dressed as an academic, in a frock coat and dress shirt with lace cuffs. Gerda swayed her hips beneath a red ruffled dress and a Spanish mantilla. Alberti wrapped himself in a white sheet and placed escarole on his head as his laurel crown. The photographer Walter Reuter smoked his pipe in a lieutenant's Cuirassier uniform. The poster designer José Renau posed as a bishop, with his hairy legs showing beneath his robe. Rafael Dieste acted as the evening's master of ceremonies, pulling all the strings. They were so completely engrossed in a childlike battle, armed with nutcrackers and paper balls, that when the nightly air-raid siren sounded, it caught them all by surprise. Everywhere they went, they were surrounded by death. This was their way of defending themselves from the war.

The entire city was a huge trench of barricaded streets filled with bomb craters. One wasn't allowed to walk down Calle de Alcalá, Calle de Goya, Calle Mayor, or Gran Vía. And on streets like Calle de Recoletos or Calle de Serrano, which ran north-south, one had to follow the arrows on the sidewalks pointing east. People were also warned not to cross plazas from their opposite ends but to travel around them, staying close to the doorways in case they needed to run inside for cover. Rules that were adopted by General Miaja when he stood in front of Madrid's Defense Council. That were stuck onto a bulletin board beside the entrance to the Alliance for everyone to see. Although several weeks had passed since the city had begun its evacuation to Valencia, its problems with provisions supplies still persisted, and the *Madrileños* had to stand in long lines for rations and groceries. But at the theaters and movie houses, it was business as usual. The Rialto, Bilbao, Capitol, the Avenida . . . A city under attack could not lose hope. They all went to see *China Seas* at the Bilbao, without knowing that the worst was waiting for them on Calle de Fuencarral on their way out. But after the typhoons, Malaysian pirates, the coolies, and the faraway gunfire of that celluloid China, the real war was not as impressive. Jean Harlow was somewhere near a yellow river of muck, and her only hope was the distant sound of a horn from a mysterious ship. Dreams.

The Alliance was the front's cultural center. In the late afternoons, the rooms on the first floor became the improvised offices for the magazine *El Mono Azul*, which aimed to lift the combatants' morale, while in the game room, the theater company Nueva Escena, directed by Rafael Dieste, staged plays set in wartime. Dinner was served at nine o'clock at a grand table lit by candelabras. The menu rarely included anything but the miserable ration of beans that was allowed, but the silverware, Bohemian crystal, and Sevres porcelain were exquisite.

At night they'd stay up late, listening to live music and to poets with feverish eyes reciting verses until the dawn began to color the bombarded nights of that heroic city pink. Gerda and Capa soon became everybody's favorite couple. They started to feel at home in the world within the Alliance, while in Paris they had never stopped being refugees, foreigners living on borrowed time. Even with their strained Spanish, they'd join the chorus to sing, with more bravado than anyone in the room, the songs of the Resistance:

> *They laugh at the bombs*
> *They laugh at the bombs*

They laugh at the bombs
Mother of Mine
the Madrileños
the Madrileños . . .

With deep voices and their hearts in the right place, they'd become immersed in Spanish humor, which could be so crude at times. Capable of laughing when their dinner plate was empty, or when Santiago Ontañón told them that the beans had worms that looked you straight in the eye, or when the poet Emilio Prados felt like singing *"La Marseillaise"* with an Andalusian accent, or when Gerda would say she smoked *yerbos* instead of *yerba*, the correct way to say "grass" in Spanish, or when Capa, in all seriousness, would start a conversation with one of the *marquesas* in the paintings.

"And why, if I may ask, did you become a revolutionary, Señor Capa?" asked María Teresa León, Alberti's wife, imitating the dusty voice of one of those Old Regime ladies adorning the walls.

"For decorum, *señora marquesa*. For decorum," he responded.

The Alliance was his Spanish home, his only family.

Sometimes the North American writer Ernest Hemingway would drop by, wearing his beret and the metal-rimmed glasses of an intellectual. He was working on a novel about the Civil War, and everywhere he went, he'd bring an old typewriter. He was usually accompanied by the *New York Times* correspondent Herbert Matthews, one of the most perspicacious reporters in Spain in those days, and Sefton Delmer, from London's *Daily Express*, who was close to six-foot, corpulent, ruddy-complexioned, and who looked like a British bishop. The three formed a curious trio of musketeers that Capa would soon join, after the time he arranged a paella dinner for everyone at Luis Candelas's caverns beneath the Arco de Cuchilleros.

In turn, Gerda was the Alliance's star. Her magnetism seduced everybody. That radiant smile and her capacity to imitate any accent and speak five languages, including *Capanese*, as Hemingway liked to call Capa's strange lingo. She'd leave the Alliance early in the morning on foot, leaving the martyrized remnants of the National Library behind her so she could walk in the direction of Cibeles. From there, she'd continue by car from Alcalá or Gran Vía on her way to the front. She'd work all day, leaning over those who were on the verge of death and who had arrived in the trenches of the Hospital Clinico, just a few hundred yards away from the bars on the edge of Madrid. Gerda, working her camera like an assault weapon. Capa saw how she changed the script that was their lives, leaning up against a barrier while shots were being fired in her direction, her nostrils flared, her skin moist with sweat, the adrenaline shooting out of every pore, her mouth shut, intensely looking around between each shot.

Each time they'd risk their lives more. But they were so young and good-looking and with a confident sportsmanship quality about them. Nobody ever thought to worry. They had a godlike aura around them. The soldiers would turn hopeful when Gerda arrived, as if her presence served as a talisman. If Little Blondie— the sobriquet they used for her—was around, things couldn't turn out so bad for them that day. Months later, when they ran into Alfred Kantorowicz again in Madrid, he confessed that while he was in La Granjuela, he'd never seen his fellow brigadists as clean and fresh-shaven as they were when she was close by, roaming around with her camera. There would be a constant scuffle in front of the mirrors and the water fountains. The foreign correspondents would fight over who would offer her their seat or who could take her in their vehicle. André Chamson invited her to climb on board the confiscated limousine they'd allocated him. She would offer them all that peculiar smile of hers, both affectionate and ironic at the same time, but without abdicating a thing. While she strolled with

General Miaja through the Alliance's gardens, he presented her with April's first rose. Sometimes she liked to chat with Rafael Alberti in the manor's library. She showed the poet how to develop his first photos in the building's basement, where they had set up a small lab. Even María Teresa León adored her with that mixture of motherly instinct and feminine rivalry.

In public, she had an enchantment that drew everyone to her. It was what Capa had admired about her from the beginning, but now he wasn't so sure of himself. He began to doubt everything. Their relationship had gone back to being what it was when they first met. Soul mates, inseparable comrades, colleagues, partners. And sometimes—just sometimes—they'd sleep together. It was apparent that, as a couple, they had retreated to the innocence of a neutral territory. But he was much too proud to be anyone's secret lover. He couldn't stand it anymore. When she entrenched herself behind that wall of independence, or when in a large group she had a private conversation with someone else while he was at her side, he'd start telling jokes in a loud voice that even he didn't find very funny, prisoner to a strange loquaciousness. Behaving the same way every time he felt ignored. He'd read into each and every one of her gestures as if it were a secret code. He suspected that she had replaced him with another. Once, he saw her standing in the vestibule, grabbing Claud Cockburn, the *London Worker* correspondent, by the lapels while she laughed and laughed about something he whispered in her ear. For days he'd do nothing but follow the journalist, trying to make his life impossible. But what in hell was she trying to pull? He no longer trusted Gerda's shows of affection; stroking his hair when she passed by him or leaning on his shoulder when they happened to find themselves sitting next to one another. Either she's with me or she's against me, he thought.

But the more he fought it, the more obsessed he grew with her body, the flat surface of her stomach, the fine curve of her ankle, her protruding clavicle. That was his only geography. He didn't need to sleep with her just one night but every night, throw her face-up onto one of those canopy beds, open her thighs, and enter her, tame her at her own pace, until she lost control, until he could soften the sharp arrises she'd sometimes get on her face, causing her to appear so distant. Just as the wind polishes the surfaces of bare rocks. That's how it was the last time. Rough, violent. They both fell to their knees, his head beneath her shirt, the salty taste of her fingers in his mouth just before letting his desire take hold of him. He grabbed her by the hair and jerked her head back, his features contorted, furious, voracious, with kisses that turned into bites, and caresses that bordered on scratches. Making ferocious love to her, as if he hated her. But what he hated was the future.

"I'm leaving," he said, eyes downward, not looking at her, just before leaving her room.

It was the only thing he could do. He was going mad.

Besides, she knew how to manage very well on her own.

She was more concentrated on her work than ever, accustomed to getting up early and coming home with the last flicker of light in the sky. In the mornings she'd travel through the Parque del Oeste and the intricate system of trenches dug up all around Ciudad Universitaria. Coming back from the front, she would walk along the grand Avenida del Quince y Medio, swerving around the pedestrians, automatically dodging the corpse of another unfortunate citizen. Desensitized to death, with a scab that had slowly formed without her knowing it, during the course of almost a year of war. She stopped short to stand in front of a movie poster. There was Jean Harlow, a woman half-bad, half-good, part-angel, part-vampiress, like any other character susceptible to surrendering. And beside her, Clark Gable, her savior, smiling, wicked, tender, the man who should put her to the test, split her in two, humiliate her a little, undervalue her, and at the same time respond to her love with a love as fierce and of the same nature. The same old story. All that interior violence and complication to defend themselves from the very tenderness. Cinema, and its tribute to dreams and shadows.

In mid-March the rebels launched a new attack on Madrid from the northeast. But the Italian troops sent by Mussolini were met with a large counteroffensive that resulted in a Republican victory in Guadalajara. Gerda visited those conquered territories, traveling through narrow roads full of mud and activity, surrounded by a large caravan of trucks and combat cars. That day she returned to the Alliance looking drained and tired, her tripod bag full of holes from Fascist gunfire.

When Rafael Alberti saw the danger she'd been in, he became alarmed, and she responded to him by pointing to her tripod stand and saying:

"Better here than in my heart." Though she wasn't too sure about that.

She ate with everyone downstairs, as she normally did, and when they were finished, they turned on the radio and listened to Augusto Fernández's report on the war. It was undoubtedly all good news. The Battle of Brihuega had been one of the Republicans' clearest victories up until then. They decided to throw a party in the hall of mirrors, but Gerda didn't want to go. Everyone insisted: Rafael Dieste; Cockburn, who never missed an opportunity to try and woo her; Alberti; María Teresa León; everyone . . . But she refused with a tepid smile. She went up to her room, staying up late to carefully mark her negatives instead. Her style wasn't like Capa's, using a wedge-shaped cutout, but using a sewing thread, just like film directors. Working with her hands helped relax her. She felt an unsettling feeling in her soul, like a yellow river of muck shrinking in the night. Since Capa had left, she was no longer interested in socializing.

Jean Harlow in *China Seas*.

Chapter Twenty-two

It was a clear day with few clouds. April 26. The temperature warm, not overly hot. A good market day with chickens, cornbread, children playing marbles, and bells ringing. The first plane appeared at four in the afternoon, a Junkers 52.

After the Fascists' defeat in Guadalajara, Franco turned his strategic focus on the Basque country's industrial belt in order to ultimately take control of its iron and carbon mines. General Mola was stationed in Vizcaya with 40,000 men for the northern campaign. But then the Condor Legion's aerial attacks began under the command of Lieutenant Günther Lützow of Hitler's army.

Four Junker squadrons in triangular formation, flying very low, backed by ten Heinkel 51s, along with other Italian reserve planes circling Guernica's sky like phantoms. First, they released regular bombs, 3,000 aluminum projectiles that weighed two pounds each, followed by a cluster of 550-pound incendiary bombs. Then, to top it off, a pack of fighter planes grazing over the center of the city, shooting down anything that moved.

It was impossible to see anything within that black smoke. In the end, they blindly bombed the entire area. For three intense hours, it rained iron, houses ablaze. An entire village burned down. "First Total Destruction of a Defenseless Civilian Target by Aerial

Bombing," declared *L'Humanité*'s headline. There had never been anything like it. Capa read the news at a kiosk in Place de la Concorde.

He was there to meet Ruth for breakfast. He hadn't seen her since his return from Spain and he needed to talk to her about Gerda. He was still haunted by lingering feelings from their last night at the Alliance. The way she avoided making any type of commitment, appearing detached. All those unanswered questions only amounted to the most intolerable feeling of uncertainty. Completely fragile, as if everything was on the brink of no return. The night before had been hard on his liver. In the beginning, he wandered through the *quais* of the Seine, his hands in his pockets, kicking stones, lost in his thoughts, and not understanding a thing. Later, he went into a bar by the pier and within the hour became completely drunk. Whiskey. No ice, no soda, without any foreplay. Each one of us has our own way of healing from a secret loss. Only when the bottle had reached the load line did he distance himself from it. His movements were slower, his heart and groin had stopped hurting him, and Gerda Taro went back to being just one more Polish Jew he could meet on any boulevard in that corner of the world that was Paris. Not any smarter, not any prettier, not any better. Just like his thoughts, the bar's contours had begun to tilt to one side, little by little. Everything was slightly out of focus, as in his best photographs. The loneliness, the melancholy, the fear of losing her . . . He swore to himself never to fall in love that way again. And he stuck to it. Of course there were other women. Some of them very beautiful, and he always appeared attentive and enthusiastic in their presence, living up to his reputation of being a charmer, but never with any ties or commitments of any kind. He preferred to entrench himself in the memory, keep it far away from the rest of the world, as if allowing someone else to enter their secret grotto would be a terrible betrayal to himself. One night in the future, after many years had passed, and when Europe was starting to climb out of the hole of the Second World War, he was actually able to seduce Ingrid

Bergman. He was in the Ritz's lobby with his friend, the writer Irwin Shaw, and the two of them decided to send the actress a dinner invitation that no intelligent woman would be able to decline. They wrote it quickly, laughing all the while, on a cream-colored paper with the hotel's letterhead:

Att. Miss Ingrid Bergman

> *This is a collective effort. The collective consists of Bob Capa and Irwin Shaw.*
>
> *We had thought about sending you flowers with this note inviting you to dine with us tonight, but after consulting the matter further, we realized that either we pay for the flowers, or pay for the dinner, but we could not pay for both. After the votes were cast, dinner won out by a wide margin.*
>
> *It has been suggested that if you were to care less about a dinner, we could send you the flowers. As of now, a decision has not been made on the matter.*
>
> *Flowers aside, we have a load of dubious qualities.*
>
> *If we continue writing, we won't have anything to talk about, since our supply of charm is limited.*
>
> *We'll ring you at 6:15.*
>
> *We don't sleep.*
>
> *Signed:*
Expectants

It was his way of staying alive, to take everything as a bit of a joke now that nothing really mattered to him. But what's certain is that he would never love anyone as much as he loved that Polish Jew with the mocking smile that not even round after round of double whiskeys could erase. He had gulped them down in one shot, one after the other, without taking a breather, while the waiter set the chairs on the tables and swept up the floor.

By now, the alcohol had worn off completely. He woke up that morning to urinate and was taken aback by his horselike spring. All he had left was a jackhammer inside his head, pounding at his temples. That's why he called Ruth. A woman was always better at seeing the light at the end of the tunnel; women can see farther, know each other well, and know what has to be done, damn it.

"Gerda's like that. Since she was a little girl, she's put up a protective shell around herself. Give her time," advised Ruth, unaware that time was the only thing Gerda did not have left.

With downcast eyes, Capa listened. Keeping quiet, imagining Gerda as an adolescent just as she had appeared in a photo he'd closely studied that she kept in a box of quince candy with other memories.

She was sitting on a dock with her shorts on, with her blond braids, holding a fishing rod, her bare feet hanging off the wharf, with the same frowning obstinacy and arrogance and headstrong attitude between her eyebrows. "The mother who gave birth to her," crossed his mind, and he had to hold his breath so that the tenderness wouldn't win. Ultimately, he blew all that air out at once, the way someone would if they were annoyed or making a fuss.

It was at that moment that he got up from his seat in a daze and crossed the square toward the newsstand. His face froze. When you're completely absorbed in your own pain, you couldn't care less about the rest of the world. Except that what he saw wasn't the rest of the world, but Spain, flesh of his flesh. A city completely razed to the ground and covered in rubble. Guernica. Each projectile thundered within his entrails.

"Jesus fucking Christ!"

That same day he negotiated his trip with *Ce Soir* to Biarritz and from there took a light aircraft headed to Bilbao.

Once again, that clear blue sky beneath the engine's turbulence, but with a coastline below that was outlined in black. The German planes continued to bomb the trenches along the slope of Mount Sollube, and Francoist tanks relentlessly advanced along the highways. But the situation in the interior of the besieged city was worse. Capa could see women and children rising out of the ruins like dusty ghosts, the sun beating down on the disemboweled building stumps, and that smell of a city bursting with dead bodies, decaying under the debris, a smell that sticks to your skin for days although you try to scrub it away with soap. Impossible to forget. Like the faces of the mothers in the port of Bilbao. They were standing there, in a starving, bomb-ridden port, saying good-bye to their children with small suitcases while they prepared themselves to board French and British ships that had to break the blockade in order to evacuate them. Biting their lips so their little ones wouldn't see them cry, re-combing their hair and buttoning their jackets all the way up so they'd look their best. They knew they would never see them again. Some of them were so young that their older brothers, five or six years old, had to carry them, still in diapers, in their arms.

Capa looked from side to side, as if he could no longer shoot any more photos. His hands were tense. He sat down on a pile of sacks alongside the reporter Mathieu Corman. He preferred the battlefield a thousand times over. They remained there awhile, the two of them, smoking cigarettes, utterly speechless, contemplating the black water while the ships moved farther out to sea.

He thought about the impossibility of transmitting what one feels in the presence of something like that. Death wasn't the worst of it, but that strange distance that crawls inside your soul forever like an irreparable chill. He saw himself leaving Budapest when he was seventeen, a pair of shirts, double-soled boots, baggy pants, and nowhere to go. The Leica wasn't big enough to photograph that. He needed a camera that could capture the movement, a film camera. A still camera wasn't enough to transmit the children's voices, the ships sailing off, the women standing on the piers until sundown, without there being a way to yank them out of there, still thinking they can see the tiny dots of the ships on the horizon. The dampness that caused the gangway to feel slippery. The immense, shadowy surface of the ocean.

It was Richard de Rochemont, director of the documentary series *March of Time*, who gave him a chance to try out a movie camera the last time he'd been in Paris. He was a friendly and reasonable man, Harvard-educated, and he wound up teaching Capa the basics of working the camera. Which led to offering him a job, and a small cash advance, to go and film war scenes in Spain to include in the series. It was a small Eyemo camera, easy to work with. Plenty of film projects and documentaries were being made about what was really happening in Spain during those years. Geza Korvin, Capa's childhood friend, was filming all of Dr. Norman Bethune's blood transfusions in hopes of raising money in Canada. And Joris Ivens, married to a female friend of his from Budapest, had begun filming *The Spanish Earth*.

In those days of mud and stars, movies were the big temptation.

That's how Gerda saw him when he appeared in Puerto de Navacerrada, wearing a thick, black cable-knit sweater, with the Eyemo on his shoulder. She also had something to show off: a shiny new Leica, bought during her last trip to Paris. Her most valued treasure.

She walked slowly toward him.

"How are you?" Her voice insecure, her heart pounding in the vein of her neck.

"How do you want me to be?" He smiled, looking confused, running his fingers through his hair. "I feel like shit."

He moved closer to her. Causing her to think he was going to take her in his arms, but he limited himself to gently passing his index finger over her forehead, parting her bangs, then quickly removing his hand. A slight gesture. They remained standing there, inches apart, slightly smiling, a hint of slyness on their faces, then serious again, looking intensely into each other's eyes with surprise and terror, witnesses to a simultaneous wonder that passed through them every time they found one another again.

Outside of Segovia, the Republican army had just launched an offensive under the command of General Walter, and what Gerda and Capa wanted more than anything was footage of a major victory. They worked side by side, swapping her Leica and his Eyemo, accompanying the troops to the front line. Under a gray sky, the soldiers moved between the pine trees, stomping on the dense lumpiness of the earth with their boots, trying to rid themselves of the morning chill. They filmed the maneuvers of the combat vehicles, the armored cars shifting their cannons from left to right as they advanced, officials talking on the phone inside a military tent as they studied a topographical map splayed on a sawhorse table, sappers alongside a pile of shells marked with yellow chalk scribblings on their sides. But neither of them had any film experience. They used the Eyemo as if it were a photo camera. First focusing on an image, then a long sweeping shot over it, as if they were blowing up stills. In the end, very few shots could be used for the *March of Time* series, although a few excerpts turned out to be very helpful for the novel their friend Hemingway was writing, titled *For Whom the Bell Tolls*.

The Republican troops weren't successful, either. The attack was a failure, and Gerda and Capa returned to Madrid, once again, without the images they had wanted. But the environment had already taken hold of them: the light over the countryside beneath the last ray of sun, the handkerchiefs of the women repairing a path where a mine had blown, the dark blue light of the foothills, the smell of coffee in the camp at daybreak within the ring of enemy mountains in the background. Capa gazed at it with nostalgia, anticipating the day he'd have to leave the country for good. It had occurred to him to think of Spain as a kind of mood, a ghostly part of his memory where Gerda would remain forever fixed, and which he'd never be able to completely abandon.

They were days of hard work and despair: losing battles, the death of friends, General Lukacs had just been defeated on the Aragon front, the struggles from house to house in the suburb of Carabanchel. They'd arrive at night at 7 Calle del Marqués del Duero exhausted, wanting nothing, and without time to think of themselves. Only a Republican victory could take them out of that rut they found themselves in.

At the end of June they headed south of Madrid, toward an area close to Peñarroya, where the Chapaiev Batallion had their headquarters. When Alfred Kantorowicz saw Gerda approaching with her camera hanging from her neck and a rifle on her shoulder, he smiled and went inside his tent to change his shirt. He hadn't forgotten about her since the day she made her grand entrance at the Ideal Room café in Valencia.

Her presence had that immediate effect on men. She awakened their most basic instincts. That same day, before her camera, the soldiers re-created a small battle that had occurred a few days back in La Granjuela. They needed to record footage for the documentary, and with the Eyemo in their hands, it wasn't so easy to choose between being a reporter or a film director. They didn't see anything wrong with staging the maneuvers of a historical event. However, the rush they experienced from something live was still much stronger. The next day they followed the troops to the front line. Their position was extremely dangerous. Gerda threw her camera over her shoulder, and before the admiring eyes of the brigadists and Kantorowicz's swearing in Aramaic, she covered those 180 yards that separated her from the trenches, in broad daylight, without anybody covering her.

"I was no longer satisfied observing all that was happening from a safe place," she wrote that night in her red notebook. "I prefer to experience the battles like the soldiers experience them. It's the only way to understand the situation."

The situation. She worked and never took a break, traveling to Valencia soon after to cover the Anti-Fascist Intellectuals Congress. It was the first time that writers and artists had united in a country at war to express their solidarity. More than two hundred attendees from twenty-eight countries. The air-raid sirens sounded all through the night. André Malraux, Julien Benda, Tristan Tzara, Stephen Spender, Malcolm Cowley, Octavio Paz . . . But when she finished her report, she returned immediately to Madrid, back to the old manor on Calle del Marqués del Duero. Whatever it took, she had to photograph a Republican victory. She was risking her life more each time, bordering on irresponsibility. Capa saw her crouched next to a militiaman barricaded behind a rock, her tiny, agile body, her head slightly thrown back, her eyes shining very bright, the adrenaline of the war galloping through her veins. Click. Another time he photographed her next to a boundary stone on the highway marked "PC," as in the Partido Comunista. The initials had nothing to do with the Communist Party, but they found the coincidence funny. She was sitting with her knees bent on top of his army jacket, leaning over the boundary stone, resting her head on her arm, her black beret, her blond hair radiant in the sunlight. Click. The war had released a new depth to her, tragic, no different from any Greek goddess. So beautiful that sometimes she almost didn't appear real.

A detailed map of Madrid was tacked up on the wall of his room. Capa was packing his bags with the radio on. According to their agreement with de Rochemont, he had to return to Paris to deliver the footage. A car was waiting for him outside the Alliance. Since he didn't have a lot of things, he took his time organizing them in his luggage. A clean shirt; some dirty ones, placed into a side pocket with a zipper, along with a few pairs of underwear. Then his black wool sweater and a pair of khaki pants, followed by his shaving cream and razors packed inside a separate leather case. He picked up John Dos Passos's book about John Reed so he could bring it as well, but at the last minute he reconsidered.

"I'll leave it with you," he told Gerda. He knew that Reed was her all-time hero.

When he was finished, he walked up to her and remained quiet, feeling awkward. With his hands in his pockets, he shifted quickly from side to side, eyeing her with those Gypsy eyes, with a defenseless seriousness on his face, similar to abandonment.

"I love you," he said softy.

And then she observed him, silent and reflective, as if she were working out an idea in her head that was too complex. I hope something will suddenly happen that can save us, she thought. I hope we'll never have the time to betray one another. I hope we'll remain untouched by tedium, or lies, or deception. I hope I can learn to love you without hurting you. I hope habit doesn't cause us to deteriorate, little by little, comfortably, as with happy couples. I hope we'll never lack the courage to start again . . . But because she didn't know how in hell to express all those real and confusing and loyal and contradictory feelings that passed like flashes through her head, she limited herself to giving him a strong hug and she kissed him slowly, opening his lips, searching for his tongue deep inside, with her eyes half-shut and her nostrils quivering, stroking his disheveled hair, while he allowed himself to be delicate and sullen and the sunlight filtered in through the large window of the Marques Heredia's old manor, and on the radio someone sang an old *copla*: "Not with you, nor without you, do my ills have a remedy, with you because you kill me, without you because I'll die."

With his travel bag hanging from his shoulder, he said goodbye to everyone downstairs in the vestibule. Promising to come back soon, shaking hands, repeating his favorite jokes . . . Masculine and somewhat coarse.

Everyone protects themselves from emotions as best they can. But when he came upon Ted Allan, he gave him a hard and frank pat on the back. The young man had just returned from the front two days ago, thinner than ever, with that withdrawn expression of shyness on his face, and that clumsy gait of a colt.

"Promise me you'll take good care of her, Teddy," he said.

To the east of Madrid, more than 100,000 Spaniards were on the verge of killing one another in the war's bloodiest battle.

Chapter Twenty-three

She appeared different, younger. She was lying facedown on the bed wearing a man's military shirt with big pockets. Her chin resting in one hand and a book in the other, slowly turning the pages. There are people who weren't born to accept things as they are, she thought. Figures lost in a world that never lived up to their standards. Individuals who don't always behave according to codified morals but to certain laws based on chivalrous ethics, people who face the world head-on, fighting in their own way, the best way they know how, against hunger, fear, or war.

Fear never held back John Reed. On the contrary, it was his natural element. When it came to reporting his stories, he would always arrange it so he could arrive at the most complicated areas. Once he was caught by surprise on the Riga front when German artillery began firing. A projectile landed a few yards away from where he was positioned, and everyone took him for dead. But a few minutes later, he was spotted walking in the middle of a dense column of smoke and dust, partly deaf, with his hands in his pockets. Gerda realized she had spent the last five minutes in a trance, staring at the paper's pores, caressing the skin of the cloth binding, as if she were sailing across a faraway sea. Afterward, she turned the page and found a photograph that Capa had left as a bookmark on page 57. She picked it up and held it up to the oil lamp so she could study it closer:

A plump naked baby lying on a sofa. Its eyebrows full and dark, its skin tan, eyes enormous and black, the color of carbon, and so much hair on its head that it looked like he could already be in high school. Gorgeous enough to eat with a spoon. There are photos that contain all the possibilities of a future within them. As if there was no other purpose to life but to confirm those freshly formed traits: the Gypsy smile, the skeptical forehead, the lucky sixth finger. The back of the photo had a date: October 22, 1913. Gerda smiled. Another one who didn't conform to things just as they were. How about that, another one.

She was restless throughout the night. She dreamt that the two of them were walking through a market in Paris, very early in the morning, with that translucent light from when they first met and the war had not yet begun, and she dreamt of being Greta Garbo, and he carried Captain Flint on his shoulder . . . She slept as if her life depended on it, or perhaps as if she wished to change her life so that it would push her far beyond those scarce opportunities. She tossed and turned in bed, from one city to the next, passing through exasperating autumns, and cried in her dreams with her eyes closed, her left knee tucked under her stomach, lying diagonally across the bed. Until she awoke with the first oblique ray of light over her pillow and the clock set on her hour.

The one of truth.

June 25, 1937. Sunday.

"When I think about all the extraordinary people who have been killed during the course of this war, it seems that one way or another, it's unfair to still remain alive," she wrote in her notebook that morning.

It had been a few days since the Republican army under the command of Líster had launched a strong offensive in Brunete at a crossing for the main supply routes used by Franco's troops stationed in Casa de Campo and Ciudad Universitaria. The attack caught the Fascists by surprise and the militia was able to quickly advance toward Quijorna and Villanueva de la Cañada. But in no time, the rebels received massive reinforcements, and in the middle of a plateau baking at 100 degrees Fahrenheit in the shade, the battle began.

Nobody was exactly certain which territories they controlled, or who controlled each *pueblo*, or which part of the *pueblo* was theirs. So they fought house-to-house. There was so much confusion that sometimes bands would accidentally bomb their own positions. Houses burning in the sun, tanks maneuvering through the streets, Fascist sympathizers positioning themselves in windows, narrow alleyways closed off, targeted bell towers, French and Belgian volunteers advancing through a wheat field . . .

What was being printed in the newspapers only confused the situation even more. To Franco, the battle had been won, while the Republicans still hadn't given up. Gerda harbored hope for a victory. She wanted those photos. Whatever it took.

"I can't carry both the Eyemo and the Leica, Ted, I need you to help me," she told her guardian angel over the phone. It was around eight in the morning. "I got hold of a car. Come on, Teddy, please say yes . . . Just this once. Tomorrow I return to Paris."

Who would have been capable of saying no? Especially Ted Allan, who would have given her the moon on a silver platter if she asked him to. There was barely any vehicle activity on the highway. From Villanueva de la Cañada and on, not even a dust cloud in the distance. Decayed rocks and pumice stones, fields of stubble, a midsummer silence that stretched across the fallow land. Bad sign. When their French driver refused to go any farther, they had to continue on foot through the wheat fields. It wasn't the type of terrain you associate with an ambush, but within that golden wheat, several men could remain hidden and completely out of sight. Around one in the afternoon, they arrived at General Walter's campsite. He was a Polish Bolshevik with square shoulders and with experience in the Red Army's strategies during the Russian Revolution. When he saw them approaching through the wheat fields, undulating like vapors in a desert mirage, their cameras in tow and their shirts drenched in sweat, he was ready to tell them to turn right back.

"Are you two crazy, or what?" he shouted at them with a harsh expression on his face, before he began ranting and raving about journalists and the mothers that birthed them. "Five minutes from now this is going to be a living hell."

He was only off by thirty seconds. Time enough to hand them each a Mauser for whatever was to follow. In no time, Francoist artillery opened fire and ten Heinkel medium bombers covered the sky over the Castilian plain. An interminable day lay ahead; bombs were suddenly exploding everywhere, and everyone barricaded themselves wherever they could while rebel aircraft dove low, riddling that corroded land with shrapnel. Gerda and Ted threw themselves into the first shallow dugout they spotted. The cordite smell in the air was sickening. German fighters swooped down to strafe the field without mercy.

"We have to get out of here," Ted screamed, leaning on her shoulder. It was impossible to hear anything above the din. "They're going to sear us."

Flashes, short bursts followed by longer ones, rattling all over the ground, snapping against rocks, explosions resonating in their eardrums.

Gerda stretched open her mouth so the noise wouldn't damage her hearing. Through her camera lens, she saw the war in black-and-white and never stopped shooting. This helped sharpen her concentration and keep her fear at bay. At one point, the reflection of the sun bounced on the metal rim of her camera, and it must have caught the attention of a biplane fighter that took a nose dive toward their position. She was fascinated by that sinister bird's vertical route that looked as if it were about to crash into the ground.

Ted instinctively covered his head with his arms, but she stuck out half her body to capture the image of the dust trails the bullets' impact had left a few feet aboveground . . . Raa-ta-ta-ta-ta-ta-ta-ta . . .

"If we get out of this, I'll have something to show the Non-Intervention Committee," she said, lying on the ground, changing the roll with haste. Her face contorted by the sun, her teeth clenched, those agile fingers working. They were the best photos of her life.

But Ted snatched the camera out of her hands. His lungs hurt from breathing in all that smoke; he stifled his cough as much as he could.

"Forget about it—we have to get out of here before they blow us to pieces." He tried using the Eyemo as a shield to protect her from the bits and shards of rock flying everywhere. He scanned the grounds around them for a safer spot. But there was nowhere to go.

The sounds of sporadic detonations were linked together by the continuous rattle of machine-gun fire and a new round of mortar attacks. The day the world ended. And then widespread panic broke out. The soldiers succumbing to panic before the deluge of artillery fire. Breaking ranks and fleeing in the direction of the highway. It was a devastating spectacle, a game of target shooting for the Fascists with their machine guns. As soon as they surfaced, they were gunned down like rabbits. There was no escape. General Walter, the head of the Thirty-fifth Division, tried his best to commandeer the combat situation, but the disbanding continued within the western sector. Gerda saw pieces of three militiamen fly through the air after a bomb exploded. It was then that she ran for cover, alone, snorting fury and humiliation, swearing in Yiddish to the god of armies, with her Mauser aimed at any Republican soldier who attempted to flee. Ted tried to hold her back by grabbing onto her shirt but failed. "They have to be stopped, can't you see they're destroying them?" she said. "Wait for me," he shouted back, reloading his rifle so he could cover her. He had never seen her so strong and sure of herself. With a gun in her hand, a torn shirt and an exposed shoulder. Impetuous, enraged, implacable, letting out wrenching screams during the last battle there was to lose. Full of rage and disappointment and an undeniable boldness of heart. As a result of their bravery, the two were able to help get the soldiers to regroup back into position.

Around five thirty in the afternoon, the planes began to retreat, leaving an empty silence over the dirt, a sense of extreme solitude in the field.

It was a miracle to have come out alive. Gerda fixed her gaze on Ted, with a mixture of gentleness and pride. Taking his face into her hands and kissing him softly on the lips. Nothing more. Barely a few seconds. For being her guardian angel.

"Thank you," he responded softly.

And though he could feel a burning flame rising to his face, he simply smiled in that way of his, both distant and timid.

The plateau was strewn with bodies and the groaning wounded who were too damaged to get up. Some were evacuated in tanks, others in blankets of canvas dragged by mules. Covered in dust, with faces blackened by smoke, Gerda and Ted began walking along the highway in the direction of Villanueva de la Cañada, listening to the sound of their own footsteps on the gravel, with a desire to remain silent out of respect for all the lives that were taken on that plateau that cursed day. In the distance, they could see farmhouses ablaze, explosions, a ravaged landscape.

An hour later and completely exhausted, the two of them continued walking as the sun was starting to set. In the distance, they heard an engine purring, and as the vehicle made its way around the curve, they could make out that it was General Walter's touring car. It was black, with a dent on its hood. They began to wave their arms in the air to capture his attention. The two of them, dying of thirst, unable to take much more. The general was not inside, and the backseat of the car was packed with wounded men, so they both jumped onto the running board and sped off.

On the way, they passed several Republican tanks and armored trucks in retreat. At one point, they found themselves within a stretch of broken terrain, with hills as majestic as medieval castles. Gerda took a deep breath and looked straight ahead, thankful for the wind on her face. She was still astonished that there wasn't a single scratch on her, thinking about the shower she'd take the minute they arrived in Madrid, overcome by that strange euphoria of the survivor, her Leica on her shoulder, her hair blowing back, thanking her star for saving her life. She had bought a bottle of champagne to say her good-byes to everyone at the Alliance. She planned to leave the next morning. That's when, in less than a tenth of a second, the car swerved, and out of the corner of her eye she could see the nose of a tank coming down on her. It was a T-26, the most powerful tank in the world. She wanted to move away from it, dodge it, but something stopped her. Its chains of iron passing over her. Ten tons of metal. The weight trapping her over her abdomen, not allowing her to move. Pulling her down, as if she were at the bottom of the lake in Leipzig and the mud had wrapped itself around her legs, forbidding her to rise to the top. She knew that she should try and relax, breathe slowly, and propel her body upward. She could almost see the lake house, with its lights turned on. And up-close, the table with white linen, a vase of tulips, and John Reed's book. She could hear screams, voices coming from far away, planes roaring high above, and the sound of Ted's voice calling out to her in a tremulous tone modulated by a sharp inflection of alarm: "Gerda, Gerda . . ." as if he were standing on a distant shore. It seemed to her that nightfall had started much too soon and that it was very cold. She tried everything she could not to drown, to push her head through the water's surface, finding it harder and harder to keep on swimming . . .

Chapter Twenty-four

Don't give up, Little Trout, you're almost there." It was the sound of Karl's voice from the shore pulling her in, while Oskar, timing it on a fob watch—ten years old, his nose covered in freckles, and wearing a striped sailor's shirt—stood waiting on the dock.

Deep below the surface, there are fantastic cities with domes made of sand and strange sparkles that shine brightly, like phosphorus in bones. Gerda felt an intense reflex of pain, so she pushed her head out of the water and felt the sun evaporating thousands of minuscule droplets over her skin.

"Come on, you're really close now . . ."

The clean sky, the water snapping with every stroke, the smell of the cedar pier baking in the sun, the coolness on her back, the pressure of the swimsuit's red elastic straps over her shoulders, that way she shook her head from side to side to dry her hair, spattering water.

The nurse resoaked the sponge in the bowl and passed it over her forehead and neck to refresh her. She was at the El Goloso English hospital, El Escorial.

"And Ted?" she asked. "Is he all right?"

The nurse nodded with a smile. She was a blond woman with very blue eyes and a face as round as rustic bread.

"And very soon, you too will be all right," she answered. "Dr. Douglas Jolly is going to operate on you. He's our best surgeon."

In the distance, Gerda saw a rectangular light in one of the large windows of that old Jesuit monastery they'd brought her to. But the pain became unbearable again; the tank had destroyed her stomach, puncturing all her intestines.

"It would be nice to have my camera."

They used two stretchers to bring her to the operating table, but she lost consciousness again before they arrived.

It was nighttime and the darkness up there was the color of prunes. She could feel her brothers' arms holding on to her shoulders as they walked along a road in Reutlinger. She could smell the wool from the sweater sleeves. Three little children, interlinking arms over shoulders, looking up at the sky. From there, they fell, two by two, three by three, like a handful of salt, those stars.

A star is like a memory—you never know if it is something you have stored or lost.

She came to with the whir of the ceiling fan, thinking it was Capa blowing onto her neck the way he did after lovemaking. They had brought her back to her bed. All she had on now was a gray shirt, her bare arm extended over the sheet. Looking extremely pale and a lot younger.

Gerda asked them to open the window so she could hear the night sounds. Her pulse rate was very low. She had seen far too many people die to feel any fear, but she would have liked to have had him close. Capa always knew how to calm her. He'd once expressed that same thought to her. At the start of the war, as they were lying on the grass in each other's arms.

"If I were to die at this very moment, here, just how we are right now, I wouldn't miss a thing," he'd said. She was leaning over his chest and she could see the lump in the center of his neck, nut-like, rising and falling each time he swallowed saliva. She wanted to touch it with her fingers. She'd always loved that part of him, protruding out like a rocky peak. Within the light of the olive trees, the color of his skin had begun to slowly change, while his body had acquired the compact texture of the earth and its rocks. She liked that protrusion a lot, like a daisy's yellow center. She needed to sleep. Feeling so tired that all she wanted to do was rest her forehead over that part of his neck, as if she'd found an opening in a tree.

The blond nurse came over to her again with a first-aid kit. Then she tied a band around her arm and used her nail to break open the top of a glass vial. Click. It sounded just like a camera taking a shot. Gerda felt the prick of the needle going into her vein. She opened and closed her hand several times for the effect to work faster, and before she could rest her head back onto her pillow, the wrinkle of her brow had already disappeared. Her expression became sweeter, slower-moving. She did not have a world that she could go back to. Every absorption of morphine into her body opened another door through which she could drift toward the future. She discovered that she was gifted with three-dimensional vision, with a clear perception of time. As if life's every moment could be reduced to an intangible point lost in infinity. That's when she realized he'd always be at this point, without ever abandoning her. It wasn't something she understood through knowledge or beliefs, but with another part of her intact brain instead. Because perhaps it is dreams that can create the future or whatever it is that comes next. It was within this realm of clairvoyance that she saw him standing there, with his shirt open, holding his head in his hands, pressing down hard on his temples, while he read the article in *L'Humanité* that stated: "The first female photographer dies in a conflict. The journalist Gerda Taro was killed during a battle in Brunete." She could suddenly see all of it, and just a few seconds later, she knew that when Louis Aragon confirmed the news in his office at *Ce Soir*, he'd clenched his fist exactly as he did, before smashing it against the wall with all his might and breaking his knuckles. And she saw him crumble at the Austerlitz Station when the coffin arrived, being cared for by Ruth, Chim, his brother, Cornell, and Henri, and continued to follow him along with tens of thousands of other people, a majority of the members of the Communist Party, who accompanied the procession in time to Chopin's "Funeral March" on an intemperate morning with a lead-colored sky, from the Maison de la Culture to the Père Lachaise Cemetery.

She also saw her father there, kneeling before the coffin, beginning the Kaddish, the Hebrew prayer dedicated to the souls of the deceased, in a deep voice, like the song of a ship's siren calling to her in the distance. Hebrew is an ancient language that contains the solitude of ruins within. Capa noticed a cramp in his back when he heard it. A type of tickling sensation over a part of his memory in which she was returning from the front covered in dust with the cameras to one side and the tripod slung across her shoulder.

He was finding it hard to keep his composure with that music of the Psalms. That's why he didn't try and defend himself afterward, when the ceremony had finished and Gerda's brothers confronted him. They blamed him for her death, accusing him, at the top of their lungs, of getting her involved in the war and of not knowing how to protect her. It was Karl who threw a vehement straight punch at his jawline. And he allowed himself to be punched, without lifting a finger, as if that beating helped redeem him of something. He also blamed himself for having left her alone, for not being at her side on that terrible last day. There was not a single minute that passed where he wasn't tortured by the guilt, so much so that he came to the point of locking himself in his studio for fifteen days, refusing food, without wanting to talk to anybody.

"The man who walked out of there at the end of those two weeks," would later write Henri Cartier-Bresson, with his Norman shrewdness, "was a completely changed person, ever the more nihilistic and dry. Desperate."

Nobody thought he'd come out of it. Ruth began to fear the worst when she saw him wandering through the Seine's quarters,

drinking until he lost all sense of reality. But Gerda knew he'd recover, like a boxer up against the ropes, knocked out, who, at the
last minute, finds the strength he didn't know he had, and he lifts
himself up and grabs his camera again, and returns to the war because he no longer knows how to live any other way. He does not
want to do it, either. And back to Spain, until the final defeat; the
Allied landings on the beaches of Normandy, with Company E
of the 116th Infantry Regiment, on the first wave, on Easy Red;
the paths of death toward Jerusalem in the spring of 1948, when
Ben Gurion read Israel's Declaration of Independence; columns
of Vietnamese prisoners advancing with their hands tied behind
their backs in the Mekong Delta, Indochina. Growing more tired,
less innocent, thinking of her every night, although he meets other
women, and even woos some as beautiful as Ingrid Bergman. After
all, he was a man. From the darker side of her memory appeared the
trace of a complicit smile on her face when she recognized him in
the lobby of the Hotel Ritz next to his friend Irwin Shaw. The smile
was so natural that the nurse thought Gerda was awake. That damn
Robert Capa, she murmured in a low voice.

She saw all of it in less than a second, and she also lifted a
glass of champagne with him one day in 1947, on the second floor
of New York's Museum of Modern Art, when he and Chim and
Henri Cartier-Bresson and Maria Eisner celebrated their founding
of the Magnum Photos agency. How she wished she could have
been there!

But the closest she felt to him was on that road in Doai Than, a
few miles outside of Hanoi. Capa had already spent too much time
destroying his liver, drinking until he was numb, doing the impossible so he'd get himself killed, sick of living without her. The heat,
the humidity, dingy hotels full of bedbugs, the golden light over
the rice fields during a late-day sun, a fisherman's fragile balancing
pole teetering through a field, the mollusk-like hats of women on
bicycles peddling barefoot over dirt roads, the youthful green of the

mountains, a gold needle on top of a pagoda, a cold thermos of tea, the humming of planes, the ubiquitous Viet Minh soldiers, moving within the tall, overgrown reeds. He jumped out of the Jeep on his way to take the final shots for a report entitled "Bitter Rice," like the film by Giuseppe de Santis. Slowly, without overstepping, he climbed a small hill of fresh grass so he could photograph a pack of men advancing from the other side of the dyke with the light in back of them. When suddenly, just as he was pressing down on the shutter, click, the world blew to pieces. In Doai Than. Hanoi.

Gerda felt the shards of shattered bone from his feet scattering like gravel through the air. Pure phosphorus. His skull resting on her ribs, the metacarpus of his left hand inside her right hand. His pelvic bone united to her trachea with the utmost intimacy. Calcium phosphate. It was then she realized that everything that lives fits into a thousandth of a flash across the firmament, because time does not exist. She opened her eyes again. It was five o'clock in the morning. Irene Goldin, the blue-eyed nurse, attentively went over to the foot of her bed.

"Have they found my camera yet?" Gerda asked with what remained of her voice.

The nurse shook her head no.

"Too bad," Gerda said, "it was new."

Author's Note

In January of 2008, three boxes filled with 127 rolls of film and unedited photos of the Spanish Civil War, belonging to Robert Capa, Gerda Taro, and David Seymour (Chim), appeared in Mexico. Some 4,500 negatives. The filmmaker Trisha Ziff came upon the boxes by way of the descendants of a Mexican general named Francisco Aguilar González, who had served as a diplomat in Marseille in the late 1930s, helping anti-Fascist refugees escape. The material is currently being studied at the International Center of Photography in New York. Practically every newspaper hailed it as a huge event in the history of photojournalism.

The story begins with the *New York Times* publishing one of those photographs found in Mexico. I'm referring to the one of a very young Gerda Taro asleep on a narrow hotel bed in Robert Capa's pajamas. If it weren't for those pencil-thin eyebrows, she could almost look like a boy. Her body sideways, her hand tucked under her chest, her hair short and tousled, her left leg bent back with the fabric gathered around her knee, as if she had been tossing and turning before falling asleep.

The figure of Robert Capa had already captured my attention long before. His photographs have always held an honorary place in my library, alongside Corto Maltese, Ulysses, Captain Scott, the rebels aboard the *Bounty*, Heathcliff and Catherine Earnshaw, Count Almásy and Katharine Clifton, John Reed and Louise Bryant, and all my other tired heroes. On more than one occasion, I thought about writing something about his life. It seemed to me that Spain owed him at least a novel. To the two of them. And I was so certain of it that it felt like an outstanding debt. But sure enough, the time hadn't arrived to pay it off yet. One never chooses these things. They happen when they happen.

In addition to photo archives, there were certain books that were of great help to me during the research phase before the writing. The first was Richard Whelan's biography of Robert Capa, as well as Alex Kershaw's gripping essay *Blood and Champagne*. To recreate the atmosphere of Madrid, Valencia, and Barcelona in those days, with their political and romantic intrigues, I found Paul Preston's *We Saw Spain Die* to be a useful reference. With great precision and detail, Preston was able to show the transformation of all those who had arrived to watch the events. And who inevitably wound up trapped by their fascination for the last romantic war, so to speak, or at least the last in which you could still choose sides. The journalist Fernando Olmeda's magnificent nonfiction book on the life of Gerda Taro was also crucial. *Gerda Taro, War Photographer*, was published by Spain's Editorial Debate, and helped to partially offset the difficulty I had accessing direct source material on the photographer in German, due to my limitations in that language. Olmeda's book gathers a large amount of data and testimonies by the German writer Irme Schaber, the author of the only exhaustive biography of Gerda Taro to date, and that, lamentably, has not been translated into any other language. It is certainly she who deserves the credit for having rescued one of the twentieth century's bravest and most intriguing women from oblivion.

This novel also owes a lot to my journalist and war correspondent friends. Through their lives, their chronicles, and their books, I was, thankfully, able to comprehend that one-way airline tickets do exist, and that a war is a place from which nobody ever completely returns. They know who they are and the extent to which they appear in this story. With it, I also want to pay homage to all the deceased messengers, men and women, who have lost and continue to lose their lives each day to practice their profession. So that all of us can find out how the world woke up that morning, as we calmly enjoy our breakfast.

As for me, I tried to honestly portray all the episodes of lives that were lived to the limit, without overlooking the darker and more polemical periods, such as the one surrounding the famous photograph "The Falling Soldier." All of the episodes that have to do with the Civil War are real, and are documented, as well as the proper names of the writers, photographers, brigadists, and militiamen that appear throughout the book. The rest—addresses, family memories, reading materials, etc.—have been re-created with the liberty that is the privilege of the novelist.

I would have liked to have reflected the intensity and complexity of those convulsive years with the skill and passion that Robert Capa, Gerda Taro, and David Seymour transmitted in their photographs. But I lack that kind of talent for working a camera. So I was left with no other choice but to attempt to travel the distance between images and words with my own weaponry and in the way I know best. Each does what they can.

Lastly, nobody is the same person when they start a novel and finish one. In a certain sense, as with any war experience, this book also represents a place of no return in my life as a novelist. There's a part of me that will forever remain in those violent war years of bombarded dreams in which Gerda Taro awoke tender and in pajamas.